Since you Arrived

THE RAIDER BROTHERS

D. E. Haggerty

Also by D. E. Haggerty

Smuggler's Hideaway Series

Before It Was Love

After The Vows

While We Waited

All Along

Beyond The Hate

The Raider Brothers Series – a Smuggler's Hideaway Spin-off Series

Until It Was Real

For The Promise

From The Start

Only for the Season

Since You Arrived

After You Returned

The Cash & the Sinners Series

How to Date a Rockstar

How to Love a Rockstar

How to Fall For a Rockstar

How to Be a Rockstar's Boyfriend

How to Catch a Rockstar

The *Winter Falls* Series

My Forever Love

Forever For You

Just For Forever

Stay For Forever

Only Forever

The *Winter Falls ~ Dempsey Sisters* series

Meet Disaster

Meet Not

Meet Dare

Meet Hate

The *Winter Falls ~ Bragg Brothers* Series

Bragg's Truth

Bragg's Love

Perfect Bragg

Bragg's Match

Bragg's Christmas

The *Love will OUT* series

A Hero for Hailey

A Protector for Phoebe

A Soldier for Suzie

A Fox for Faith

A Christmas for Chrissie

A Valentine for Valerie

A Love for Lexi

The *Love in the Suburbs* series

About Face

At Arm's Length

Hands Off

Knee Deep

Other romantic comedies by D.E. Haggerty

Molly's Misadventures

Chapter 1

Zane – a man who's about to receive a package that will change everything in his life

ZANE

A hum of excitement fills me as I finish packing my bag. It's been way too long since I've gotten away from my hometown island of Smuggler's Hideaway. But the wait is over. Tomorrow I'm off on a trip to drive a motorcycle through South America.

I wish I could drive my own motorcycle, but I'll have to settle for buying one in Colombia. My brothers would lose their collective minds if I was gone longer than the two weeks I've already planned, which means driving my own bike is out.

My brothers and I own and operate *Buccaneer's Whiskey & Distillery*. No matter how many times I explain to them how I can do my job as marketing manager while on the road, they won't listen. Leaving me stuck in the office way more often than I want.

The doorbell rings. I've been expecting my brother Miles. He's picking me up on his way to the *Rumrunner* bar, where we're going to celebrate my younger brother, Kai, and his girlfriend, Harper, being together.

I don't understand the appeal of tying yourself to one woman for the rest of your life – I prefer a smorgasbord of women – but Kai's happy and his happiness is what matters.

"I'm coming. Hold your smugglers!"

I fling the door open and smile at Miles. Except it's not my brother on my doorstep. It's a beautiful woman. I dial up the smile and flash her my dimples.

"Why, hello, beautiful."

She rolls her eyes. "You don't remember me, do you?"

I rake my gaze over her body. "Maybe I need a refresher."

Forget about going to *Rumrunner* to watch Harper humiliate Kai. I prefer a warm, naked body in my bed. I open the door and motion her inside.

"Do you want to come in?"

"No, but she will."

She will? My brow furrows. There's no one else on my porch.

"She? Who?"

She reaches down to pick up her bag. Wait. This isn't a bag. This is a baby car seat. And it isn't empty. An actual baby is sleeping in it. The woman tries to hand the car seat to me but I toss my hands in the air and back up.

I have no idea what's going on but I am not accepting a baby from a virtual stranger. Let's face it. I'm not accepting a baby from anyone other than my family. And, even then, I have to be bribed. Other babies? No way. No how.

"What exactly is going on here?"

"I didn't realize you were this slow. You certainly weren't slow in bed."

I scowl. I can be slow in bed. I just prefer not to. Fast and furious is way more fun in my opinion. But how does she know about my preferences in bed?

"Have we met before?"

She sighs. "It's a good thing you're pretty because smart you are not."

"I'm not stupid."

"Let me give you a refresher. Yes, we've met before. Yes, this is your baby. And bye-bye."

She sets the baby car seat back on the ground and whirls around to escape. I catch her wrist before she can flee.

"What the hell? You can't leave me a baby. I don't even know your name."

She spits daggers out of her eyes at me. "Do you sleep with so many women, you can't remember all of their names?"

Technically, I never sleep with women. I undress them, give them an orgasm or two, and then leave. Sleeping isn't involved.

I scratch my neck. "I suck at remembering names."

"Could you be any lamer?"

I'm getting annoyed. I didn't make this woman any promises. I never do. I'm always clear. A night of fun with no strings attached. Nothing else is on offer. And it never will be. Settling down is not on my agenda.

"I'm sorry, I don't remember you. Why don't you come in and we can discuss this?"

"There's nothing to discuss. Adele is your baby. I'm done raising her on my own. You're up."

"How do I know this…," I clear my throat. "…Adele is mine?"

She plants a fist on her hip. "Are you saying I'm a slut?"

"How the hell would I know if you're a slut? I don't know who you are!"

"Don't you dare yell at me in front of the baby," she hisses.

I inhale a deep breath. I'm not one to yell at people. Especially not a woman I don't know. Or, at least, don't remember. I'm usually laid back and easygoing, but this situation is not usual.

"Let's start over. I'm Zane, and you are?"

I hold out my hand and she stares at it for a few long moments before finally placing her hand in mine.

"Daisy."

"Hi, Daisy. It's lovely to see you again."

"I wish I could say the same," she mutters.

I ignore the jab and nod to the baby. "And this little girl is yours?"

"Ours. She's ours."

I grit my teeth before I lash out. I might enjoy playing in the sheets with women but I'm always careful. Always. Babies are not on my agenda. I have no interest in becoming a parent.

"I always use protection. You're certain Adele is mine?"

"I'm certain and now I'm done with this conversation."

She whirls around to leave again and panic strikes. She can't leave this tiny creature behind. I have no idea how to handle a baby.

"You can't abandon your baby with me."

"She's your baby, too."

I have no idea if this baby is mine, but denials aren't getting me anywhere.

"You can't abandon our baby with me."

"You're up. I'm done being a single mom. I'm done missing out on all the fun. I'm done with missing classes."

Classes? She must be a college student. I rack my brain for memories of any women I've slept with who were college students, but I come up empty. I don't spend a whole lot of time talking to a women about their lives when I seduce them.

"I'm sorry you're having a difficult time. Let's discuss this. Let's figure out a solution."

"I have the solution. Daddy's going to raise Adele. Discussion over."

My heart stutters as my chest tightens. I can't raise a baby. I can't be a dad. I have no idea how.

"I can't handle a baby now. I'm leaving tomorrow to drive through South America." Even in my panic, I know better than to claim this baby isn't mine.

"Too bad. I've cancelled plans for the past four months. You're up."

"Four months? Is she four months old? What else can you tell me about her?" Maybe if I keep asking Daisy questions, she'll change her mind.

"You'll figure it out."

"Figure it out?"

She starts backing up. "The way I did."

"But…"

I don't get a chance to finish before she sprints to her car. I chase after her but the baby screams. I stare at her for a second before I swear and reach down to pick her up.

"Shush, baby. Don't cry."

I rock her in my arms and she immediately settles. Phew.

"What am I going to do with you?" She stares up at me with big blue eyes. The same blue eyes I gaze into every morning in the mirror.

Shit. Is this baby mine? What am I going to do?

I do the same thing I've always done when I need help. I go in search of my brothers.

Chapter 2

Sloane – a woman who's always late but it's never her fault

SLOANE

I roll over in bed and snuggle into the blankets. My dog whines.

"Five more minutes, Boozer boy."

The mix between a Golden Retriever and a Great Dane licks my face, and I shove him away.

"Knock it off. It's not time to get up yet."

My alarm blares. Bummer. It is time to get up. I slap the alarm clock to shut it up. An alarm clock is old-fashioned, but since I have the tendency to throw blaring items across the room in the morning – I am not a morning person – a cheap alarm clock works best.

I shove Boozer off me and roll out of bed. I stretch my arms into the air before bending over to touch my toes. There. I've exercised for the day.

Boozer sticks his snout under my hand. "Does someone need extra loving this morning?"

I kneel down to pet him and he immediately rolls over onto his back. His tail thumps on the ground as I scratch him.

"Who's a good boy? Who's my good boy?"

Boozer jumps up to lick my face. "There's my baby."

Don't ya just love dogs? Dogs are reliable and trustworthy. Unlike men.

"Come on. Let's have some breakfast."

Boozer rushes out of the bedroom. He slips and slides as he runs down the hallway to the kitchen. I'm not as fast as I follow him. I feed him before settling at my tiny kitchen table with a cup of coffee.

My phone beeps with a message.

Where are you?

I frown. Why is Lana, the mayor of Smuggler's Rest – the largest town on the island of Smuggler's Hideaway where I live – messaging me?

At home. Where else would I be?

You forgot. I knew you'd forget.

Forget? What could I have possibly forgotten? Today is my day off. I only set my alarm because I'm tired of cleaning up Boozer's mess if I don't let him out early enough. I don't have anywhere I need to be. I—

Damn. I did forget. I promised to help out at the *Mermaid Lagoon Race*. Only in Smuggler's Hideaway would people shove themselves into glittery mermaid tails, attempt to swim in them, and call it a festival.

Supposedly, it celebrates the island's 'heritage' – smugglers hiding their loot on the island during Prohibition – but mostly it's an excuse to drink questionable moonshine before noon and argue about whether mermaids are real. (They are. Ask anyone who's had three shots of moonshine and seen the sunrise.)

I'm on my way.

I jump to my feet. My elbow hits the table and my cup of coffee wobbles. I try to grab it but it tips over before I reach it. Coffee spills all over the table. I slap a hand down to stop it but all I succeed in doing is burning my hand.

"Ouch!"

Boozer barks.

"Shush, baby boy," I admonish as I rush for a towel. There aren't any hanging in the usual spot – probably in the wash – so I reach for a paper towel. Only to notice the roll is empty.

"Figures," I mutter as I whip my shirt off to use as a towel.

Once I've mopped up the mess, I throw the t-shirt in the overflowing hamper – I'll get around to doing the laundry one of these days – before jumping into the shower. Boozer whines and pokes his snout into the shower.

"I'll walk you before I go to work."

He stares at me with his big, brown eyes. "Don't make me feel guilty for working. If I don't work, there's no doggy kibble for you."

He barks before settling on the bathroom mat to wait for me. There's no such thing as privacy when you have a dog.

Once I'm dressed, I hook Boozer up to his leash. I open the door and he tries to rush outside. I hold him back so I can peek into the hallway first. Good. There's no one around.

It's possible I lied to my landlord about having a dog. It's not my fault. I didn't have a choice. There aren't many apartment buildings on Smuggler's Hideaway that accept dogs and I may have been kicked out of those. I can't help it if Boozer gets excited when he meets other dogs.

We run down the hallway to the stairs. I know. I know. I shouldn't let Boozer walk down two flights of stairs. It's bad for his hips. But it's better than him peeing in the elevator. Trust me. The smell of dog urine is impossible to mask. My nose wrinkles at the memory.

We exit the apartment building and I exhale a sigh of relief. We made it.

"Aha!" Melanie – aka the bane of my existence – shouts as she rushes around the corner.

I startle and Boozer howls in response. I scratch behind his ears as I allow my heart rate to settle.

"I knew you were hiding a dog in there!"

I have to tread carefully here. Melanie works in the mayor's office. The last thing I need is for her to tattle to the mayor on me.

"I'm not hiding a dog."

She points to Boozer. "What's that?"

Boozer growls in response and I tighten my hold on his leash. He doesn't usually snap at people – he's more a lover than a fighter – but Melanie isn't usual people. She's a prude who enjoys ruining everyone else's fun. She needs to find a new hobby.

"Boozer isn't my dog. I'm dog-sitting."

It's not completely implausible since I'm known for doing all sorts of odd jobs around the island. I work as a bartender at *Rumrunner* full-time but in the winter, when the tourism slows down, I need to supplement my income.

Melanie crosses her arms over her chest and purses her lips. It's not a good look on her. "If you're dog-sitting, why have I seen you with this beast for the entire year you've been living in this building?"

I shrug. "Because I dog-sit for him more often."

"You're lying. And once I prove you're lying, I'll tell the landlord."

"There's no reason to tell the landlord since I'm not lying." I'm also not crossing my fingers behind my back. Lie. I'm totally crossing my fingers behind my back. It never hurts to hedge your bets.

She narrows her eyes. "I heard your dog barking and thumping his tail this morning."

"I told you. I'm dog-sitting." There. I didn't lie this time. Go me.

She wags her finger at me. "One of these days, your lying is going to get you in trouble. And I'll be there to witness it."

I beam at her. "How nice you want to witness me living my life."

My phone beeps. Uh oh. It's probably Lana asking where I am. "It was lovely seeing you. But I'm in a hurry this morning."

"When aren't you in a hurry?" she mutters as we pass her.

I ignore her snarky comment. No good can come from my response. Besides, I've hit my limit of lying for the day and it's not yet ten o'clock.

And it's possible she may be correct. I am always in a hurry. But it's not my fault. I have a lot going on in my life. Hurrying is a necessity.

I make my way to the beach with Boozer. I hope I don't get kicked out of my apartment because the proximity to the beach is awesome.

I keep a tight hold on Boozer's leash as we meander toward the water. My phone beeps again. Oops. I forgot all about the earlier message.

I dig my phone out.

You're late.

I start to respond but then Boozer barks and yanks on the leash. I tighten my grip and dig my heels into the sand, but he's stronger than me. Way stronger.

"Boozer, no."

He lunges anyway, muscles straining, tail wagging at the rabbit twitching his nose at him from the dune grass.

"Don't you dare."

He dares.

The leash jerks, and I go flying forward. I release him at the last second before I face-plant. Sand fills my mouth and my nose.

Boozer tears off in hot pursuit.

Thirty minutes later, after chasing him through most of the island's beaches and muttering threats of obedience school, I finally knock on Pam's door. Pam dog-sits Boozer when I have to work. She opens it, takes one look at me – hair wild, shirt covered in sand, mascara smudged like raccoon eyes – and her mouth drops open.

"I can explain."

Chapter 3

"Motorcycles don't come with baby seats."

ZANE

I place the baby in the carrier.

"Okay, baby. We're going to my brothers. They'll know what to do."

I have five brothers – Eli, Rhett, Jaxon, Miles, and Kai – who have always been there for me. Ever since the day my dad left us when I was eleven, I've relied on them to help me solve my problems. And if ever there was a problem I needed help solving, this is it.

I march toward the garage but come to a screeching halt in front of my motorcycle. I can't exactly put a baby seat on the back of my bike.

"Shit."

I debate calling one of my brothers to pick me up, but this isn't news I want to share more than once. Ride share it is.

"Hey, Trent," I greet the doorman of *Rumrunner* ten minutes later.

Rumrunner is a speakeasy complete with a hidden door down an alley you wouldn't otherwise notice. Tourists have to solve a riddle to enter, but locals don't. It's also where Kai's girlfriend, Harper, works and where my brothers have gathered tonight to watch Harper's grand gesture to Kai. Daisy couldn't have picked a worse night to drop a baby on my doorstep.

"Are you carrying a baby?"

Does he think I'm carrying a doll in the baby seat?

"Is it your baby?"

I growl. Adele isn't an 'it'.

He holds up his hands. "Whatever. Go on inside. Take your baby into a bar. Great parenting."

I freeze. I don't want to be a parent. But maybe bringing Adele here was a bad idea. Maybe I should call my brothers and ask them to come outside.

"Zane!" Miles waves at me. "What are you waiting for? A personal invitation?"

Too late to escape now.

Harper and Kai are kissing on the stage while some Taylor Swift song plays in the background as I enter. I guess the grand gesture is over and they've moved on to the loving portion of the evening. Good for them.

I don't want a relationship, but I'm happy for my baby brother. He's been mooning over Harper for months. I'm glad they worked things out.

I make my way toward my brothers. Rhett has his arms wrapped around his fiancée, Dakota, as they sway to the music while Jaxon and his wife, Blossom, whisper to each other.

"Where are Eli and Paisley?" I ask Miles since he's the only brother not involved with a partner.

"They're staying home with Stephanie."

Eli's girlfriend, Paisley, recently had a baby girl. I'm not surprised they stayed home. My oldest brother turned into an overprotective brute the second Paisley announced she was pregnant.

"Why are you late?" Miles points to the baby seat. "And what prank are we pulling?"

Adele lets out a wail and his eyes widen. "You brought a real baby as a prank? This is going to be epic."

I scowl. "Adele isn't a prank."

Although, I can understand why he'd think she is. I've been pulling pranks on my brothers since I figured out how to lock the inside of a closet door.

His brow wrinkles. "Are you babysitting? Dude." He shakes his head. "I didn't realize the lengths you'd go to for a woman."

Honestly, I don't have to do much to get a woman. Crook my finger, show them my dimples. Not much else needed.

Adele lets out another wail. I jiggle the baby seat but she continues to cry. Great.

I unbuckle her and lift her into my arms. I sway her from side to side, but she doesn't calm down.

"What is happening?" Rhett asks.

"Is there a baby in Zane's arms or am I hallucinating?" Dakota asks.

"If you're hallucinating, then so am I," Blossom says.

"Why are you holding a baby?" Jaxon asks.

Kai and Harper hurry toward us. "Whose baby is this?" Harper asks. "Do I need to contact the police to report a lost baby?"

I open my mouth to answer but I lose my train of thought when the bartender stomps toward me. Sloane has always been off limits to me. She's older and is friends with my brothers and their friends.

All of which equals messy. And I don't do messy. Or commitment. Or relationships.

But her being off limits doesn't stop my pulse from increasing when her breasts bounce as she makes her way through the crowd. Her dark brown eyes narrow on me, and her light brown hair with streaks of blonde in it flies behind her. She reminds me of a revenging angel.

Except I have no interest in stripping down an angel. But what I wouldn't give for one night with Sloane. Off limits, I remind myself.

"What are you doing to this poor baby?" she asks before snatching Adele out of my arms.

"What's wrong, sweetie pie?" She coos to the baby. "Do you need to be changed?" She lifts her up and sniffs her diaper. "Nope. No need to be changed. You must be hungry."

Sloane switches her attention to me. "When did she eat last?"

"I don't know."

She blinks. "You don't know? How can you not know?"

I stuff my hands in my pockets and shrug. I'm not explaining to this woman, I yearn to spend a night twisted up in the sheets with, how Adele was dropped on my doorstep thirty minutes ago.

She rolls her eyes. "Typical." She snags the baby seat before whirling around and marching away.

I start after her but Miles stops me. "What is going on?"

"Not here."

"Come on." Harper motions me toward the back hallway. "We can discuss this in my office."

I trudge behind my brothers as we make our way through the crowd to her office. When we arrive, Sloane is on the sofa feeding Adele.

"Where did you get a bottle to feed her?" I ask.

"It was in the bag in the baby seat."

"What in the hell is going on?" Rhett asks before shutting the door behind him.

"I…" My gaze lands on Sloane, and I trail off. I'm not embarrassed of being a player, but I don't want her to know about the baby.

She waves at me to proceed. "I'm going to hear all about it via the smuggler's grapevine anyway."

She's not wrong. The islanders are dead serious about gossiping. Keeping a secret on the island is next to impossible.

I swallow. So much for resolving this situation before everyone on the island finds out. "A woman showed up on my doorstep, claimed Adele is my baby, and left."

Miles whistles. "Dude."

"Some random woman?" Jaxon asks. "You didn't know her?"

My face warms. "She said her name is Daisy, but I didn't recognize her."

"Figures," Sloane mutters.

Another reason why I will never touch Sloane. Her opinion of me isn't great.

"Are you certain she's your baby?" Jaxon asks.

"She has the Raider blue eyes."

"You should have a paternity test done to be certain," Blossom says.

I'm hoping to resolve this situation before a paternity test is needed. I keep the thought to myself and make some non-committal noise. It must work since my family drops the subject.

"What are you going to do?" Dakota asks.

"Find Daisy and give her back her baby."

"Do you know who Daisy is? Do you have her last name? Where she lives?" Rhett throws questions out at me.

"No."

He whips out his phone. "I'll get Eli on the case."

I've never been more thankful that my oldest brother is a billionaire. Over the past year since he's been back home, I've learned how much money can help solve 'difficult' situations.

"What are you going to do in the meantime?" Dakota asks. "You're not going to drop her into the foster system, are you?"

She was raised in the foster system. In fact, they have two foster children they've adopted. As much as I wish I could call a social worker to handle Adele, I won't. I don't shirk my duties. I'm not my father.

"Do you want us to take Adele? We have everything we need for a baby since we have Mira."

I should say yes. It's the easy and logical response after all. But when I look at Adele, I can't fathom letting someone else care for her. It's irrational. I don't even know if she's mine.

"Nah."

Dakota studies me for a moment before nodding. "We'll bring you over some supplies to get you through the night."

"Thanks."

"In the meantime," Sloane stands, "it's time for daddy to burp the baby."

Daddy? I'm no daddy, whether or not I'm the biological father to this baby.

I hold up my hands and retreat a step. "But you're doing such a good job."

"Don't be a scaredy-cat."

She shoves the baby into my arms and I'm forced to catch her. "What do I do?" I ask as I hold Adele at arm's length.

"Put her over your shoulder and pat her back."

"Do you want me to do it?" Dakota reaches for the baby, but before she can take her, Adele burps and a stream of white liquid emits from her mouth.

I stare at the front of my shirt, which is now covered in spit-up. "Is this normal?"

Sloane giggles in response. "Welcome to parenthood."

My stomach curdles. Parenthood? I am not father material.

Chapter 4

"It's just a dog. What is everyone's problem?"

SLOANE

I wag my finger at Boozer. "Don't you dare give me those puppy dog eyes. I have to work. I can't skip another day or Harper will fire me."

His big, brown eyes are hard to resist. Unlike a particular man's deep blue eyes. Those are easy to resist, considering Zane Raider is a player.

I can't believe he has a baby. Correction – I can believe the player impregnated a woman. What I can't believe is how a woman left a baby with him. Zane and the word 'responsible' do not belong in the same sentence.

And yet somehow my entire body lit up when I saw him holding the baby. No, no, no. I am not interested in Zane. I don't care how much those bedroom eyes promise. The man's a player. He can't commit to anyone or anything.

Boozer whines again and I force thoughts of Zane away. I check the time. I need to be at *Rumrunner* in ten minutes. It's a five-minute walk. I have a bit of time.

"Okay. Fine. We'll play with the ball for a few minutes. But then I really do need to go."

He barks before running to the corner where all his toys are gathered. He picks up his ratty stuffed animal before running back to me.

"Give it to me."

Of course, he doesn't give me the stuffed rabbit. He wants me to 'steal' it from him.

"Fine."

I play tug of war with my dog until he releases the stuffed rabbit with a bark.

"No barking."

His response? Another bark.

"I'm serious, Boozer. You can't bark."

I throw the rabbit and he runs after it – barking the entire time. I sigh. This is why we don't play inside my apartment.

Someone knocks on my door and I groan. Great. Another neighbor coming to complain about my dog.

When did everyone on this island become such rule followers? When we were teenagers, we never followed the rules. We sent tourists on wild goose chases and teased them about mermaid sightings. And we never came home before it was dark.

I blame Melanie. No one else on this island is a prude. While the rest of us were skinny dipping in the ocean, she was tattling to our parents. Spoiler alert. Our parents didn't care.

My mom certainly didn't.

There's another knock on the door. Good timing. Thoughts of my mother never lead to anywhere happy.

I start for the door but then I remember – Boozer can't be here!

"Come on, boy." I grab his collar and drag him toward the bathroom. He must realize how urgent the situation is since he doesn't fight me.

I shut him inside and hurry toward the front door – and nearly trip on his stuffed rabbit. I snatch it from the floor but what should I do with it? I can hardly open the door with a dog toy in my hands. I stuff it down the sofa cushions.

There's another knock on the door. Someone's impatient.

"Coming!"

I make sure I'm wearing my bartender smile – the one that gets me all the tips – before opening the door. My stomach falls to the floor. It's my landlord, Sheena.

"Good morning."

She scowls at me.

"Do you want to come inside?" I motion her in.

She scans the room as she enters. Her gaze snags on the doggy corner and her scowl deepens. I block her view and herd her toward the sofa.

"Have a seat. Shall I make some coffee?"

"Yes, please." She sits down and *squeak!* She jumps to her feet. "What in the world?"

I rush to her, but I don't manage to distract her before she yanks Boozer's stuffed rabbit from the cushions. I never should have bought a stuffed animal with a squeak inside of it.

"What is this?" She squeezes it and it squeaks again. Boozer barks in response.

"I knew it," she mutters as she hurries toward the bathroom.

I block her. "What are you doing? You can't inspect my apartment without my prior approval."

"Unless you've violated your rental agreement, which you clearly have."

"I have not!" Do I sound indignant? I'm trying my best here.

Boozer barks again and I bite my tongue to stop myself from cringing. I had to fall in love with a barking dog? I couldn't fall in love with a dog that's quiet?

Sheena points to the bathroom door. "And you don't have a dog in here?"

"I'm dog-sitting."

She crosses her arms over her chest and glares at me. "You've been dog-sitting for several months, according to the neighbors."

Neighbors? Ha! It's one neighbor in particular, and her name starts with M and ends with Melanie. I should have pushed her in the swimming pool in eighth grade when I had the chance.

"I occasionally dog-sit to earn extra income."

"And you have an entire corner of your living room stuffed with dog toys for when you dog-sit?"

I ignore her sarcasm. "Yes."

"Enough! I have had enough!"

I bat my eyelashes. "Enough of what?"

"Enough of your lies."

"I'm not—"

She slashes her hand through the air. "Enough of you paying the rent late every month."

"I'm not late *every* month." Sometimes I forget to pay the rent. I don't understand what the big deal is.

"Enough of you forgetting to bring your trash cans inside."

Who remembers their trash cans?

"And enough of you claiming this dog is not yours." She pushes past me to open the bathroom door. Boozer runs out and hurries toward me. He sits in front of me and growls at Sheena.

"I want you out of here by the end of the business day."

My chest squeezes. I can't breathe. End of the business day?

"I can't move out in one day! How will I move my furniture and pack my things in one day?"

"Fine. You can have until the end of the week. But not one day more. Do you understand?"

"Please, Sheena. I need a few more days."

She snorts. "I'm not falling for it this time. I give you a few more days, and before I know it, months have passed and I have neighbors complaining to me every day about your dog again. I'm done."

I clutch my chest as the pressure increases. Is there an invisible elephant sitting on it?

"I'm sorry, Sloane, but I have a business to run. You're thirty-one. You need to start acting like an adult."

She swivels on her heel and marches out of the apartment without another word.

"Well, hell, Boozer. What are we going to do now?"

Chapter 5

"Nothing says Thanksgiving like a surprise baby."

ZANE

I exit the car – a car I had to borrow from a friend since I refuse to buy one – and stare up at Eli's house. It's Thanksgiving and the entire Raider clan is gathered at my big brother's house to celebrate the occasion.

I wasn't supposed to be here. I was supposed to be exploring South America on a motorcycle for a few weeks. Instead, here I am trying to figure out how to remove a baby seat from a car.

How the hell is this my life? I admit I'm a player. But I'm always careful. Always.

The door flies open and Mom rushes out. Ready or not – here we go.

"Zane, my boy." She hurries to me. "We didn't expect you today."

"Mom." I kiss her cheek.

"Why are you standing outside?"

Has she not heard about the baby yet? My brothers didn't tell her?

I glance toward the house and notice all five of my brothers are standing on the porch. Which can only mean one thing. They've started some kind of bet about how Mom will react to me having an unexpected child.

My brothers will use any excuse to start betting. When they aren't pranking each other. I'm usually part of the fun. Hell, I start the fun most days. But fun died the second Daisy dropped Adele at my doorstep.

"I'm… ah…" How do you explain you have a child you didn't know about to your mom? I motion to the interior of the car.

"Zane Raider! Why is there a baby in this car?"

She doesn't wait for an answer before reaching inside to nab the baby. "Hello, little one," she coos. "Get the car seat. We'll discuss this inside."

She hustles inside without waiting for a response. Meanwhile, I still don't know how to remove the stupid car seat.

I guess I'll figure this out on my own since YouTube wasn't any help. Eli nudges me out of the way. "I've got this. You better get inside and deal with Mom before her head explodes."

My oldest brother unclicks the baby seat as if it's nothing. "How do you know how to do that?"

He slaps my shoulder. "You'll learn."

I frown. I don't want to learn. I don't want to be a father. Moreover – I can't be a father.

"Did you find out where Daisy is?"

He sighs. "Sorry. Not yet."

Damn. I can hardly return Adele to her mom if I don't know where she lives. Something inside me rebels at the idea of giving Adele back. I ignore it. I can't be a dad.

We arrive at the porch where the rest of my brothers are exchanging money.

"Seriously?" I ask. "My life is falling apart, and you're making bets?"

Rhett growls. "Your life is not falling apart because you have a child."

"I'm not you. I don't want the fairy tale happy ending with a wife and two children."

"Then, you're a fool," he says before entering the house.

Miles chuckles. "This is not news."

"Whatever," I mutter before following Rhett inside the house with the rest of my brothers on my heels.

Paisley hurries toward me with baby Stephanie in her arms. "I'm beyond excited. Our children are the same age. They'll grow up together."

Our children? Adele isn't here to stay. My stomach sours at the thought, but I ignore it. I've been ignoring it a lot lately.

"Son," Stuart greets. "You better explain to your mother what's happening."

I bristle. I'm not his son. Stuart isn't my dad. He's my step-dad. And he didn't come onto the scene until I was an adult.

"My goodness," Mom exclaims. "Who put this diaper on this baby?"

I cringe. "I did."

"Didn't anyone ever teach you how to put a diaper on a baby?"

Miles barks out a laugh. "Remember when we had to 'care' for a baby for a week, our junior year of high school? Zane refused and ended up getting detention for a month."

"I remember. He had to sort buckets of clam shells. He came home smelling of clam for a week." Kai holds his nose.

Harper sighs. "I'm glad I wasn't in school at the same time as the Raider brothers."

Kai throws an arm around her shoulders. "You missed out but I have the rest of our lives to make it up to you."

Harper practically melts into him and I roll my eyes. Don't get me wrong – I'm happy for them – but did all of my brothers have to fall in love?

First, Eli and Paisley fell in love. Technically, they've been in love since high school, but whatever. Then, Rhett fell head over heels for Dakota. She gave him the runaround. It was fun to watch.

Next came Jaxon and Blossom. Jaxon 'fake' married her to help her out, and before I knew what was happening, they were in love and the marriage was real.

And, most recently, Kai and Harper got together. Kai took one look at Harper and was smitten.

At least Miles and I are still single. Although, Miles has been yearning for Hazel, the woman he abandoned years ago, and I fear he's about done waiting for her to stop hating him.

Dakota snatches Adele from Mom's arms. "I'll change her while Zane explains why he suddenly has a baby."

"I used to like you!" I shout after her retreating figure.

"You love me and you know it!" she shouts back.

Mom grasps my hand and drags me into the living room. "Now," she says once we're seated next to each other, "tell me why you suddenly have a baby."

"Is anyone surprised Zane has a baby?" Miles asks.

I glare at him. "You're no saint either."

He scowls. "But I'm not a player."

"Beg to disagree," Harper mutters under her breath.

"Can't an old man have a nap without being bothered?" her father, Henry, asks from the armchair where he was sleeping. Since Kai fell in love with Harper, her dad has joined our growing family.

"I warned you to go to bed early last night." Harper wags her finger at him. "But, no, you had to stay up late and binge watch the new detective series."

"I have to watch those series when you aren't around. Otherwise, you spoil the ending."

Harper shrugs. "I can't help it if I figure out who did it within five minutes."

"Who did it?" I ask even though I have no clue what show they're referring to.

Mom tuts. "You can't avoid my questions all day."

I can try. Except I can't use the exploding diarrhea excuse and hide in the bathroom when I have a little baby to care for.

"Nope." Mom grasps my hand and squeezes. "You aren't escaping with your motorcycle now."

Kai snorts. "He doesn't have a motorcycle today."

"Because he has a baby," Mom adds. "Where did the baby come from?"

I smirk. "Do I need to explain to you? You have six boys. I thought you figured it out already."

Stuart growls. "Do not tease your mother when she's concerned about you."

I open my mouth to remind him he isn't part of the family but snap it shut before I can speak. Stuart is Mom's husband. Whether I like it or not, he's part of the family. Mostly, I like it. But I'm having a hard time liking anything at the moment.

"A woman showed up on my doorstep the other day with a baby. She said I'm Adele's father and then announced she's done being a single mom and left."

Mom gasps. "She abandoned her baby?"

"She's young. I think she's a college student."

"College student?" Eli pulls out his phone. "I'll let the PI know."

"The PI?" Mom's brow wrinkles. "Why did you hire a PI?"

"To figure out where Daisy is."

"Daisy?"

"Adele's mom."

Mom growls. "You're not giving Adele back to a mother who abandoned her, are you?"

That was my plan. Give the baby back, pay monthly child support – assuming Adele is my baby – and move on with my life.

"Hold on. We don't know the baby is Zane's yet."

I nod to Rhett to thank him.

"He has the Raider blue eyes," Miles reminds everyone.

"We'll make sure anyway," Eli says. "We can do a home test, but we should do a lab test in case we need proof for litigation."

I swallow. "Litigation?"

"In case Daisy fights your claim for custody."

"Hot damn," Henry says. "I had my money on Miles being the first Raider brother to have a child out of wedlock."

"Hey!" Miles glares at him. "I always use protection."

So do I. Fat lot of good it did me.

Eli stands. "Okay, we have a plan. We'll do a paternity test and I'll make an appointment with a lawyer to discuss custody."

I don't know if I want custody of Adele. But I can't admit to it when my mom and brothers are ready to fight my battles for me.

"Does this mean we can eat? I can smell those pies from *Pirate's Pastries* from here." Henry pushes up from his chair and Kai rushes to help him.

Why couldn't Kai be the one to have a baby dropped at his doorstep? He already has a built-in family with Harper and her dad.

I'm checking the expiry date on all the condoms in my house when I get home.

Chapter 6

"Harper's never going to trust me again."

SLOANE

I stop at the back entrance to *Rumrunner*.

"Boozer, sit." I wait until my dog obeys my command before continuing. "This is a big night for me. Harper left me in charge because she's celebrating Thanksgiving with her family."

And I'm not jealous at all. Not at all. My stomach gurgles in protest. I ignore it. I don't want to be part of the Raider clan.

"I want to show her I can handle it. Once she sees how awesome a job I've done, she'll appoint me assistant manager. Which means a raise."

I desperately need a raise since I don't have the money to pay a deposit for a new apartment. Which means Boozer and I are currently between homes. It's temporary.

"All this means I need you to behave tonight."

Harper will lose her mind if she discovers I brought Boozer to work again. But I don't have a choice. Pam is away celebrating Thanksgiving with her family. And I can hardly leave my dog in the car while I'm at work.

"Let's do this."

We enter the bar, and the sound of the crowd immediately hits me. Thanksgiving is a big day for the speakeasy. Tourists enjoy visiting the island for the long weekend. And exploring the local speakeasy is a must do.

"Oh, good. You made it," Dave, the bartender, says when he rushes into the hallway. "The crowd is insane tonight."

Boozer wags his tail at Dave but when the bartender ignores him, he barks. "You brought your dog? Harper is not going to be happy."

"What she doesn't know, won't hurt her."

Dave snorts – probably because I've never managed to get away with bringing Boozer to the bar without Harper finding out – before entering the storage area.

I make my way to the office and unlock the door. I place the doggy bed on the floor and point to it. "Boozer, stay."

He whines but I ignore him. It's bad enough I brought him with me to work. I'm not letting him wander around the bar.

He tucks his tail between his balls and slinks to the bed.

"Wish mommy luck." He barks. Good enough.

I shut the door behind me and make my way to the bar where a line of customers is waiting. I join Dave behind the counter.

"Who's next?" I ask and get to work. The next thirty minutes fly by as I help customer after customer.

I scan the bar to make sure everything is under control before smiling at the next person in line. "Hi! How can I help you?"

"I demand to see the manager."

"I'm the manager." For tonight and – fingers crossed – after tonight, too. Assistant manager. Manager. Same thing.

He sneers at me. "You're the manager?"

I dial up my smile. "Yes."

"Is this some kind of joke?"

"No joke, sir. How can I help you?"

"You can get me the real manager."

"I am the real manager." I pinch myself. "Ouch! Yep. All real. No fake person here."

"Don't be cute with me and go get the manager."

Dave sidles up to me. "Do we have a problem here?"

The man points at me. "This woman won't get the manager."

"Probably because she is the manager this evening."

I knew there was a reason I liked Dave. Besides him not tattling on me when I bring Boozer to the bar.

"This woman can't be in charge."

I blow out a breath. "Okay. Now, I'm getting annoyed. Either tell me what your problem is, or I'll ask Trent to escort you off the premises."

I motion to the bouncer and he immediately marches toward us.

"You're kicking me out?"

"What's the problem?" I ask instead of explaining myself. It appears Mr. Sexist doesn't listen anyway.

He slams a glass on the bar with such vehemence, liquid spills over its sides.

"This is not moonshine."

The glass is engraved with the logo of the *Buccaneer's Whiskey & Distillery*. Underneath are the words 'Smuggler's Hideaway Moonshine'. "It appears to be moonshine."

"Moonshine doesn't burn your nostrils and scar your esophagus."

Wrong. Moonshine will totally burn your nostrils. And other things if you happen to be too close to an open flame. I swear it wasn't my fault. I didn't realize the fire was lit. Besides, eyebrows grow back.

"Smuggler's Hideaway Moonshine isn't the same as moonshine you can buy other places."

"What a crock!"

"The moonshine on the island is prepared according to recipes developed during Prohibition by smugglers."

"How the hell is that legal?"

I don't know. It just is.

"I can't answer any legal questions."

"I want my money back."

I cringe. My answer – there are no returns on drinks – will not make him a happy camper. I try another tactic.

"Why don't you order another drink on the house?"

Accept the drink. Accept the drink.

A sparkle appears in his eye and I swear under my breath. This is not going to be good. "I'll have a Ramos Gin Fizz."

Crap. A Ramos Gin Fizz requires shaking for at least ten minutes, and the line behind him is already growing after all of his complaining.

"Coming right up. I am required to warn you that a Ramos Gin Fizz contains raw eggs." There is no such requirement, but people are freaked out by raw eggs. Let's hope Mr. Complainer is freaked out, too.

"Raw eggs?" His nose wrinkles. "I've never had a Ramos Gin Fizz with raw egg before."

"Then, you haven't had a Ramos Gin Fizz. The recipe calls for egg white."

I hold my breath as I wait for his reply. "Fine. I'll have a regular gin fizz."

"Coming right up."

A gin fizz is a simple cocktail of gin, lemon juice, sugar, and soda water. It doesn't require at least ten minutes of shaking to emulsify the cream and egg white.

"Good job," Dave mutters to me when I grab a bottle of gin from the shelf.

His words warm my heart. Dave could easily fight me for the assistant manager position. He's worked at *Bootlegger* nearly as long as I have. And he doesn't have a habit of bringing his dog to work. Or being late. Or forgetting the shipment of beer is coming early.

But he's not interested in the position. I am. And I can do this. I can be the assistant manager.

I prepare the gin fizz and set it down on the bar in front of the customer. "Here you are. Enjoy."

He doesn't walk away – of course not – he sips on the drink in front of me while blocking other customers from being served.

"This is acceptable," he says and finally wanders away.

"I want to try the moonshine," the customer behind him says and I nearly groan. "Don't worry. I can handle my liquor." He winks and now I do groan.

I pour his drink and hand it to him. I'm about to serve the next customer when I notice a commotion near the entrance to the bathrooms.

"I'll be right back," I holler to Dave.

He nods and I make my way to the crowd. "What's happening?"

"There's a dog in the women's restroom."

I have a sneaking suspicion I know what dog it is. I push through the group until I reach the office. Sure enough, the door is hanging open. I hope he didn't break the door. I can't hide a broken door from Harper.

I shut the door before returning to the crowd. I bypass the line to the restroom and enter. There's a group of women gathered around an open stall.

Before I reach the stall, I can hear slurping. The kind of slurping only a dog makes. Great. Boozer is drinking the toilet water.

I grab his collar and pull him away.

"Hey!" a woman shouts. "What are you doing? You can't abuse animals this way."

"This is my dog, Boozer."

She frowns at me. "Why are you letting him drink from the toilet? There could be germs in there."

"More germs than on his asshole, which he spends at least an hour every day licking?"

Her nose wrinkles. "You need to take him to the vet."

As if I have the money for a vet.

I drag Boozer out of the restroom. "Show's over, folks!"

I set off for the office but Dave's shout stops me. "The keg for *Depth Charge Stout* is empty."

"I got it!" I respond before pivoting in the other direction.

I keep hold of Boozer as I trudge to the wall behind the bar. I tap the wall and a door opens to reveal the hidden walk-in cooler.

I quickly switch out the kegs. I've been working at bars since I was old enough to drink. I could do this in my sleep. I probably have.

"And now it's time for you to return to the office," I tell Boozer.

He barks before springing for the door. I rush toward him. "No, don't!"

But I'm too late. The pressure of his paws causes the door to shut. Damn it. The failsafe to open the cooler from the inside is broken. Whenever the door shuts with someone inside, it automatically locks itself. And there's only one person who has a key.

I dig my phone out of my back pocket.

"What's wrong?" Harper answers.

"Um… we kind of have a situation."

So much for Harper not finding out I brought Boozer to work today.

Chapter 7

"Great. It turns out the baby only sleeps if I'm holding her. So long sleep."

Zane

"Wah."

I groan and roll out of bed. The bed I've only been laying in for thirty minutes since Adele's last crying jag.

"Come on, baby girl," I murmur as I lift her from the crib.

My family saved me again. I have everything a baby could possibly need and then some crammed into my spare room. I have no clue what most of the things are, to be honest. Wipe warmer, formula dispenser? No idea what those things do.

"Wah!"

"What do you need?" I must be more tired than I thought, since I actually wait for Adele to respond. She doesn't. She's a baby.

"Do you need your diaper changed?"

Please, for the love of all pirates, do not need your diaper changed. I lift the baby up and sniff. No toxic smell.

"Are you hungry?"

She can't be hungry. I literally fed her a bottle less than an hour ago.

"What do you need, baby girl?"

"WAAAH!"

Someone is not happy, but I have no clue why. I cuddle her close and pat her back as I walk to my bedroom in search of my phone. I'll call Mom. She'll know what to do.

I pick up my phone but pause before dialing when I realize someone isn't crying anymore. Awesome. Time for more sleep for Zane.

I return Adele to the crib, but the second I set her down, she starts crying again. Damnit. Why is this so hard?

I pick her back up and rock her in my arms. "Sweet baby girl, please go to sleep. I need sleep."

She quiets down again and relief fills me. Maybe I'm not a terrible parent after all.

But when I lay her back down in her crib, she starts wailing again.

"What is it, baby girl? What do you want?"

Her response? She wails until I pick her up and rock her in my arms.

I'm not an idiot. I can figure this out. Or rather, Google will figure it out.

"Check for basic needs," I read the result of my Google search. "Is the baby hungry? Nope. Does her diaper need changing? I don't think so. Great. Now what?"

I continue to read. Try soothing techniques. Okay. What are soothing techniques? Rock, sway, or take the baby for a walk in a stroller.

"Do you want to go for a walk, baby girl?"

I glance around the room, which is now completely stuffed with baby stuff. Stuff I hope I can give back to my family once Adele returns to her mother. My stomach sours at the thought of not having Adele in my life, but I ignore it. I'm not cut out to be a dad.

"There!" I shout when I finally locate the stroller amongst the mess and Adele cries. I rock her until she quiets again.

"I need to lay you down for a second."

Adele doesn't approve of the idea. As evidenced by her wailing as if the world is coming to an end. It sure as hell feels as if the world is coming to an end with her screaming.

I get the stroller set up and place Adele in it. She continues to cry until we're moving.

I hope she falls asleep while we're walking. I'll probably fall asleep while we're walking.

I wander down the sidewalk and the wind hits me. Brr. It's colder outside than I thought. Good thing I'm wearing a sweatshirt.

But Adele isn't. Shit. Shit. Shit.

I whirl us around to return to the house. She begins howling with rage. It's as if she knows where we're going. The neighbors are going to think I'm torturing her.

I whip off my sweatshirt and wrap it around her. She snuggles into it and the screaming stops.

I continue our walk. I'm cold now since I'm only wearing a t-shirt but better I'm cold than a tiny defenseless baby.

I walk around the block. It's quiet outside. I check my watch. It's three a.m. No wonder it's quiet. All the bars and restaurants closed an hour ago.

I whistle as I continue to stroll around Smuggler's Rest. It's the biggest of the three towns on the island, but it's still a small town. In the winter months, when there are fewer tourists, it's a quiet place to live.

Which is why I was headed out to South America this week. I don't do well with quiet. Smuggler's Hideaway is fine in the summer when it's propped full with tourists – many of whom are single women searching for a good time – but in the winter, it can get boring. I don't do boring.

Although I could imagine spending a winter between the sheets with a certain bartender. Sloane won't give me the time of day, though. She thinks I'm a player. She isn't exactly wrong.

But there's nothing wrong with being a player. I don't make promises I can't keep. I simply don't make any promises.

My brow furrows when I notice a woman sleeping in her car. She has light brown hair similar to Sloane's. Hold on. It is Sloane. Why is she sleeping in her car?

I knock on the window as gently as possible but her dog pops up and begins barking.

"Quiet, Boozer," she orders without opening her eyes.

I knock on the window again. No sense in being gentle. Her dog is already awake.

Sloane's eyes fly open. When her gaze lands on mine, she slams her eyes shut.

"Sloane," I call.

She shakes her head.

I chuckle. "Are you pretending you can't see me?"

"Maybe."

"Roll down your window."

"Why?"

"Because I want to talk to you."

"Too bad. I don't want to talk."

"Sloane," I growl.

"Fine," she huffs and rolls down her window. "What do you want?"

I lift a brow. "What do I want? Are you seriously asking me what I want?"

"You knocked. I assume for a reason."

"Why the hell are you sleeping in your car?"

Her hands shake as she places them on the steering wheel. "I was falling asleep after my shift. I thought I'd take a little nap before driving home."

I point to the backseat, which is filled with boxes and suitcases. "Are you moving somewhere?"

Her eyes fall closed and she drops her forehead to the steering wheel. "Yes."

"Where are you moving to?"

"I don't know yet."

I growl. I have a sneaking suspicion I know what's happening here. And I don't like it one bit. "Are you living in your fucking car?"

She throws her arms in the air. "What business is it of yours?"

None. But I'm not letting her sleep in her car. I'm not an asshole.

"Follow me home. You can stay with me tonight."

"Boozer and I are fine here."

She shivers and I notice she has goosebumps. "You're not fine, and I'm not arguing about this."

She narrows her eyes at me. "Don't argue then. Just go away."

"You have two choices. You can come home with me."

"I am not going home with you," she snarls.

I raise my hands. "I promise to keep my hands off of you. You can sleep in my spare bedroom."

"What's my other choice?"

My stomach dips. While I would love to spend a night or two twisted up in the sheets with her, she's not interested. It's for the better. I can't offer Sloane anything more than an orgasm or two. She deserves more. She deserves everything. But I'm not the man to give it to her.

"I call Harper and you explain why you're sleeping in your car to her."

She spits daggers out of her eyes at me. "You're an asshole."

"So, I've been told."

Adele cries and Sloane scowls. "What are you doing outside at this time of night with a baby?"

"Come home with me and I'll explain."

"You're not going to let this go, are you?"

I grin. "Do I appear to be the kind of person who lets something go?"

"You appear to be the kind of person I want to punch in the face," she mutters.

"You'll have to get in line behind my brothers."

"The Raider brothers." She tuts. "If you weren't trying to sneak into *Rumrunner,* you were fighting with each other."

"Don't forget pranking each other."

"How can I forget? I nearly peed my pants when the clown dropped down from the ceiling."

"You can't blame me. No one expected you to be at the high school."

"And my reward for helping to clean out the school library was to be scared half to death."

I shrug. "At least you didn't pee your pants." The wind whips through the street and I shiver. "Come on. Let's get back to my house before I catch a cold."

"Why are you outside in the middle of the night in November in a t-shirt?"

I point to Adele. "She needed my sweatshirt more than I did."

Her face softens when she looks at the baby. What I wouldn't do to see that look on her face when she looks at me. But this woman deserves more than a night with me. No matter how much my fingers itch to touch her, she's off limits.

"Fine," she finally gives in. "I'll stay with you tonight, but you'll keep your hands to yourself, and it's only for tonight."

I shove my hands in my pockets. "Deal."

Notice I didn't promise not to figure out somewhere else for her to stay. No way is Sloane living in her car. Not if I can do something about it.

Chapter 8

"Remind me never to complain about Boozer's whining again."

SLOANE

"This is a mistake. This is the biggest mistake of my life."

Boozer barks.

"Glad you agree."

He barks again.

"You can't be barking tonight. Baby Adele needs quiet."

He whines before laying down. I swear he understands what I'm saying.

We arrive at Zane's house and I park in the driveway. I blow out a breath and pause a moment to enjoy how lovely his house is. It's a ranch with a big front porch and an attached garage. It's not huge, but it appears cozy – a home.

My stomach sours. A home. Wouldn't it be wonderful to have a home? A place with a family you can rely on. A safe place you don't have to worry about being kicked out of.

I've been trying to build a home for myself since I was eighteen. I'm now thirty-one, and I'm the furthest I've ever been from having a home. Something needs to change. But I'm not sure what or how to make change happen.

Zane motions to me from the front door. How is it possible, he looks even sexier holding a baby in his arms?

As if he needed any help in the sexy department. Zane Raider has enough sex appeal on his own with his lush brown hair that curls slightly at the ends, his piercing blue eyes, and the three-day scruff of a beard on his square jaw. Not to mention those broad shoulders that appear able to carry the weight of the world on them.

Not for me, I remind myself. Zane Raider is not for me.

I snort. Zane is for every woman. One night only.

I have no interest in a player. Which is why Zane is off limits. With a capital O to the hell no.

I open the door and Boozer leaps over my lap. He rushes to the front door and I chase after him.

Zane bends down to scratch behind my dog's ears and I nearly melt. There's something incredibly sexy about a man who loves dogs.

Knock it off, Sloane. Zane isn't your man.

"Come on in." Zane motions into the house.

I was right. His house is a home. The sofas in the living room look comfy and well-used. The oversized television attests to hours spent relaxing in the room.

"This is…" I trail off to yawn.

He chuckles. "Let me show you to your room before you fall asleep standing."

I can actually fall asleep standing. I've done it behind the bar once or twice.

Zane leads me down a hallway. We pass a bedroom I assume is his. It smells of the oaky musk he uses. There's a huge unmade bed and not much else in the room.

We continue past another open door. This room is a mess of boxes. The only piece of furniture I can make out is the crib in the corner.

We come to the final door and Zane flings it open. "It isn't much, but the bed is more comfortable than your car."

I let the car comment go. I'm too tired to explain my current living situation.

"Thanks." I scan the room. It's smaller than his, but it's an adequate size with a double bed, a dresser, and some nightstands.

Boozer launches himself through the air and lands on the bed. I cringe. "Sorry. He's used to sleeping on the bed. I'll get his doggy bed from the car."

Zane stops me with a hand on my wrist. My pulse skips at the skin-to-skin contact. I can't help but wonder. How would it feel if he were to touch other parts of my body? With his fingers? And his tongue? My stomach tingles with excitement.

I step away from him before I lose what little is left of my sanity and jump him. Bad idea. He's a player. Plus, he's holding a baby.

Zane clears his throat. "He can sleep there. I don't mind. Sheets can be washed."

I lift an eyebrow. "You know how to do laundry?"

He shrugs. "I have a washing machine. I can find directions on how to use it online."

My mouth gapes open. Is he serious? Granted, he's only twenty-five, but he must know how to use a washing machine.

He barks out a laugh. "The look on your face. I know how to do laundry."

And why is his ability to do a domestic skill sexy? Why? I must be starved for affection. There's no other reasonable explanation since I know better than to get involved with a player.

"I guess Boozer's sleeping on the bed." I yawn again. "Sorry. I closed the bar down tonight."

"Not a problem." He nudges me forward into the bedroom. "Bathroom's down the hall. Towels are inside. Get some sleep. We'll talk in the morning."

"Thanks," I mutter before shutting the door.

I faceplant in the bed. Boozer cuddles up to me. I fall asleep before I can wrap an arm around him.

"Wah!"

I awake at the sound. I blink at the darkness. Where am I? This isn't my car. Or my apartment.

Oh, right. Zane found me sleeping in my car. My face warms with embarrassment but I ignore it. There's nothing to be embarrassed about. The situation is temporary.

"WAAH!"

I roll over and cover my head with the pillow. Some little baby girl is not a happy camper.

The cries continue, but I ignore them. This is not my problem. I shouldn't stick my nose where it doesn't belong.

Boozer whines. "It's not our problem to deal with."

He barks. "Shush."

He settles with his head on his paws to stare at me with his big brown eyes. I roll over. I'm not getting involved.

"WAAH! WAAH!"

"Oh, for mermaid's sake." I roll out of bed and stomp out of the room.

Zane is pacing the living room with Adele in his arms. "Go to sleep, baby girl. I need my sleep. If you think I'm cranky now, wait until the morning."

My heart warms. Zane is utterly adorable, pleading with his daughter for a bit of sleep. It's useless, but he's adorable.

"Can I help?"

He whirls around. "Fuck. Did I wake you?" He shakes his head. "Of course, I woke you."

"Technically, she did."

"Sorry."

"No need to apologize. What's wrong?"

"I don't know. She's been crying all night. Walking her was helping before but it's not anymore."

"Is she hungry?"

"I fed her two hours ago."

"Dirty diaper?"

"She's dry."

"Is she teething?"

"Teething?" The color drains from his face. "Will she cry this way while she teethes?"

"The entire time."

He swallows. "Maybe she'll be back with her mom before then."

I blink. "You're not keeping her?"

"I'm not cut out to be a dad."

What a bunch of seal blubber. He is a dad whether he wants to be one or not. He can step up and be an adult about the situation. Or he can run away. I guess I know which direction he's leaning toward.

"Is she sick?"

"How would I know?"

"Does she have a fever? Is she having difficulty breathing? Is her skin pale or blue or blotchy?"

His mouth drops open. "How do you know all this?"

"I worked at a daycare when I was in high school."

I don't bother to add I had to work because otherwise I couldn't be sure my mom would remember to feed me. He doesn't need to know my pathetic story. Besides, he wouldn't care.

"She doesn't feel warm."

"Do you have a thermometer?"

He shrugs. "Maybe in one of the million bags Dakota and my mom gave me."

His mom and sister-in-law gave him all the supplies he needs for his surprise baby? Wow. Must be nice knowing you can rely on your siblings and mom.

"May I?" I reach for the baby but wait for his nod before touching her. I place her against my shoulder and rub her back. "Sometimes rubbing a baby's back helps."

I feel Adele's tummy rumble before she burps.

"Good girl. She just needed to release some trapped air."

"Damn." Zane runs his hand through his hair. "I forgot to burp her after her last feeding. I suck worse at being a parent than I thought I would."

"There's no need to become a drama queen. Any parent can be forgetful. Ask me about the time my mother left me at the gas station in Florida some day."

Please don't ask. I don't want to explain how my mother forgot I was in the bathroom and drove off without me. I waited at the gas station for twelve hours before she returned.

Twelve hours. It took her six hours to remember she has a daughter.

"Here." I offer him the baby. "I need to change my shirt."

"Crap. I'm sorry."

"It's no big deal. But you do need to curb your swearing around Adele."

"It's fine. She doesn't understand."

"But she will some day."

"Some day. Right."

I can practically see the wheels turning in his head. He's thinking Adele won't be around long enough to understand his swearing.

Wow. Zane is a bigger jerk than I imagined. How can anyone abandon their child?

I could ask my dad. Assuming I knew where he was.

Chapter 9

"Came up with a plan to fix Sloane's situation. What could possibly go wrong?"

ZANE

"Hey, baby girl," I murmur as I lift Adele from her crib. She gurgles at me and I nearly forget about the sleepless night I just endured.

I finally got to sleep around four a.m. after Sloane burped the baby. She came out of her bedroom, looking adoringly rumpled with her hair in a rat's nest. And took less than a minute to calm Adele.

Too bad Sloane isn't here every night.

Hold on. Why can't she be here every night? Guessing by how she was sleeping in her car, she has nowhere else to be.

Hmm… maybe Sloane is the solution I'm searching for.

By the time she stumbles into the kitchen thirty minutes later, my plan is formed.

"Morning," she mumbles as she opens the sliding door to let her dog out. Boozer rushes outside. "Don't chase any rabbits!"

She shuts the door and whirls around to face me. Holy shit. My heart gallops, and my tongue gets tied. She must have changed after Adele spit up on her because she's now wearing a tank top showing off her perky breasts and a pair of tiny shorts. Damn. I want those long, smooth legs wrapped around my waist while I pound into her.

My cock twitches in agreement. It's a good thing I'm holding Adele in my arms, or I'd have her pinned to the wall by now.

"Coffee." Her eyes are half-closed and her jaw is adorably grumpy.

Adorably grumpy? I shake my head. This is Sloane. The woman who doesn't like me.

I motion to the pot. "Help yourself."

I sip on my own coffee as she moves around my kitchen. I expected to be annoyed with a woman in my domain, but Sloane being here doesn't bother me a bit. This is a good sign that my plan will work.

Sloane sits down at the kitchen table across from me.

"We need to talk."

She holds up a finger before sipping on her coffee. She finishes half the cup before sighing and setting it down.

"There. I'm ready to speak now."

"Not a morning person?"

"I'm a bartender. Morning isn't in my vocabulary."

Hopefully, I can get her to change her mind.

"I have an idea how to solve your homeless situation."

She scowls. "I'm not homeless. I'm merely temporarily without a home."

I scratch my beard to stop myself from explaining how being 'without a home' is the definition of homeless. I want her on my side.

"I stand corrected. I have an idea on how to solve your temporary without a home situation."

She narrows her eyes at me. "You're not going to tell everyone, are you?" She huffs. "Damn it. I knew I should have parked somewhere outside of Smuggler's Rest. But I was too tired after my shift to go driving around the island."

"I won't tell anyone."

"But…"

"Why do you assume there's a condition to my promise?"

She snorts. "Because I've known you most of my life, Zane Raider. You Raider brothers gossip worse than the ladies who work at city hall."

"We don't gossip."

She rolls her eyes. "What do you call telling everyone on the island about your brother accidentally wiping his ass with poison ivy?"

"Hilarious."

She giggles. "It was pretty funny watching Kai walk around with his jeans hanging off his ass."

I pause a moment to enjoy how beautiful she is when she smiles. Sloane is always beautiful, but when she smiles, the entire room feels lighter.

"About this idea…"

She holds up her hand. "I don't need handouts."

"Good. Because I wasn't planning on giving you any." There goes my Plan B. I straighten my back and stick with Plan A. "How about you move in here?"

She barks out a laugh but sobers when she notices I'm not laughing. "You're not joking?"

"No."

Her brow furrows. "You want me to live with you? Mr. I Don't Let Women Sleep After Sex Because It Gives Them The Wrong Idea?"

I bristle. I'm not ashamed of being a player, but she makes me feel as if I should be. "I don't lead women on."

"I never said you did."

I open my mouth to argue – she implied otherwise – but arguing with Sloane won't get me what I want.

"Let me clarify. You wouldn't live here for free."

Her eyes flare. "What exactly are you proposing?"

Her dark brown eyes sparkle with interest and I fist my hands before I reach for her. Off limits, I remind myself. Sloane Wilder is off limits.

She deserves flowers and chocolates and cuddles in the morning. Not a man who impregnated a woman he doesn't even remember.

"You become my nanny."

"I thought you were giving Adele back to her mom."

That's my plan. Or it was. I don't know. Things are getting confusing. I don't try to explain to Sloane, though. She already thinks I'm a jerk.

"I'll have Adele with me for the foreseeable future." There. It's not a lie.

"I can't be your full-time nanny. I already have a job."

"You work in the evenings. I work during the day. You can watch Adele during the day while I'm at work."

"I have to be at work before most offices close for the day to help with the after work crowd at *Rumrunner.*"

"I'll make sure I'm home before you need to leave."

Her brow wrinkles. "Don't you need to work until the distillery closes?"

"I can work from home."

"In your office filled with boxes of baby stuff?"

"I'll unpack those." Or send them back to my family when Adele returns to her mother. Eli must have found Daisy by now.

Her dog barks and Sloane stands to open the door for him. He runs inside and skids to a halt in the kitchen. He plops down on his ass and whines at Sloane.

"Sorry. I forgot about your breakfast."

I stand. "Not a problem. I have some dog food left from the last time I watched Rhett and Dakota's dog, Delphine."

She finds two bowls and pours water into one while I fill the other with dog food. Once Boozer is settled, we return to our discussion.

"What do you think? Will you be Adele's nanny?"

She points to her dog. "What about him? We're a package deal."

I love dogs. But I've never adopted one because I don't want to be tied down. I want to be able to jump on a plane for the other side of the world without notice. But the spontaneity ship has sailed.

"As long as you clean up any accidents in the house, he can stay."

"Deal."

"Does this mean you'll stay and be my nanny?"

"Until I figure out somewhere else to live."

Works for me. I won't have Adele forever anyway. "Deal."

"And you let Boozer out at night when I'm working."

"I can't leave Adele alone in the house."

She motions to the backyard. "The backyard's fine."

"Any more conditions you want to discuss?"

She drums her fingers on the table and I hold my breath. I need Sloane's help. This is the perfect solution.

And you want her in your house.

I ignore the voice in the back of my mind. It doesn't matter what I want when it comes to Sloane. She's off limits.

She holds out her hand. "You have a deal."

I clasp her hand and a spark ignites at the touch. Will sparks ignite if we touch elsewhere? What if I trail my finger down her long leg? Or plump her breast? And how would it feel to sink into her? My cock twitches.

This is a bad idea. I'm inviting temptation into my house, and I've never been any good at resisting temptation.

I grit my teeth and pull my hand away. I can't give in. I need a nanny for Adele.

"Wah!"

Speaking of my baby girl, I hurry to my feet. "I'll help you move your things in later," I say as I run away.

Correction. It's not running away. I'm making a tactical retreat.

I have too much going on with finding out I'm a father – assuming I actually am Adele's biological father – to get involved with a woman. Besides, I don't get involved with women. Never have. Never will. Getting involved leads to complications.

I pick Adele up from her crib. And I have enough complications in my life.

Chapter 10

"Note to self: always check if the shower's occupied."

SLOANE

I scroll through the rental listings on Smuggler's Hideaway. There isn't much. Finding a place to rent on a small island is hard enough. But finding somewhere when you've been banned from most apartment complexes on the island? Nearly impossible.

And it doesn't help that the island is a magnet for tourists. Most property owners simply leave their rentals empty during the winter rather than renting them out to locals. They can earn way more renting to tourists for four or five months than to a local year-round.

Don't get me wrong. I love Smuggler's Hideaway. I've loved the mermaid-obsessed island ever since my mom brought us here when I was twelve. The local kids immediately adopted me. They didn't care about how many schools I'd gone to over the years. They included me.

Which is why I threw an absolute fit when Mom wanted to move on. I locked myself in the bathroom and refused to budge for an entire weekend.

Mom finally gave up. She's more of a lover than a fighter. Most hippies are.

I push thoughts of Mom out of my mind. The last thing I need is to go for a stroll down memory lane.

Boozer sticks his snout under my hand.

"Yuck. Wet."

He whines in response.

"We'll go for a walk in a minute."

He barks and leaps off the bed. He runs around in circles – his tail wagging with such vigor he nearly falls over.

"Who's my silly dog?"

I shut my laptop and roll out of bed. I tiptoe down the hallway. I peek inside the nursery. Adele is sleeping in her crib. She's not my responsibility today – it's Sunday and Zane is home – but I can't help but check on her.

I sigh as I stare at her crib. I'd love to have a child, a family. But I don't want to be a single mom. I grew up without a dad. I won't put my child through the same hardships I endured. Although I bet being a single mom would have been a lot easier for Mom if she didn't flit from job to job.

Enough with the memories. Nothing good ever comes from reminding myself of the past.

I lead Boozer down the hallway and out of the house. By the time we return thirty minutes later, I'm covered in mud from head to toe.

I glare at my dog. "I told you not to chase the poodle."

I swear, if he could shrug, he would. He's completely unrepentant. Which became pretty obvious when he mounted the poodle and refused to get off of her until I yanked him away.

I stand on the porch and lift my hand to knock. What am I doing? I live here now. Temporarily. This isn't a permanent situation. I'll figure out a place to live soon enough.

My stomach sours but I ignore it. Making a happy family with Zane and his baby isn't going to happen, no matter how much I want it to. Which I don't, by the way. Zane is a player. Enough said.

I slowly open the door and peek inside. I don't want Zane to see me covered in mud. I drop my shoes on the porch and enter with Boozer.

"Be quiet. The baby might be sleeping."

He follows me to the bedroom. I notice Adele is still sleeping in her crib, and Zane's door is closed. He's probably catching up on sleep after the hectic night.

I strip out of my muddy clothes and set off for the bathroom. I freeze at the entrance to the hallway. Shit. I'm naked. In Zane's house.

Towel. I need a towel. Where are the towels?

I run down the hallway – one hand over my boobs and the other over my crotch – toward the closet. I yank the door open. Yes! A towel. I grab it and rush to the bathroom.

I hurry inside, slam the door behind me, and lean against the wall. Phew. That was close. Note to self: Keep a few towels in the bedroom from now on.

In my defense, I'm not used to living with other people. I refuse to have a roommate. Not after my first roommate thought it would be fun to give my dog a hash brownie. Trust me. It wasn't fun.

"Hello?"

Oh my pirate. How did I not notice the shower was running?

"Is someone there?"

"There's no one here."

Zane peeks out from behind the shower curtain. His eyes widen as his gaze rakes over my naked body.

"Don't look!"

He jerks and stumbles backward at my shout. "Fuck," he mutters before gripping the shower curtain. It doesn't help. He falls into the bathtub, taking the shower curtain with him.

I rush to him. "Are you okay? Did you hit your head?"

"I'm fine," he sputters as the water hits him in the face.

I reach across him to switch it off.

"Why are you naked?"

I look down and realize my breasts are dangling over his face. I snatch my hand back and drop to my knees next to the tub.

"I… ah…" I search the area for my towel. It's at the door where I abandoned it when he fell.

I start to crawl toward it but then realize my ass is on display. I flatten myself on the ground.

"Are you slow crawling?"

"Are you looking?"

I glance over my shoulder. He's now standing in the bathtub with the shower curtain wrapped around his body. And he's staring at my ass. His deep blue eyes are filled with such passion, they're nearly violet. My nipples tighten in response. I nearly moan at the feel of my hard nipples scraping against the floor.

"Stop staring!" I try to shout but my voice comes out all breathy. I clear my throat but it doesn't help reduce the lust currently running rampant throughout my body.

"What do you expect me to do? Your perfect ass is naked in front of my face."

Perfect ass? Did Zane say my ass is perfect? I wiggle it, but stop when I realize what I'm doing.

"I expect you to be a gentleman and turn around." There. I managed to speak without my voice sounding husky. Go me.

"You want me to turn around so you can check out my ass?" He wiggles his eyebrows. "No problem."

He starts to push the shower curtain down.

"Stop!"

"You're the one who entered the bathroom when I was in the shower."

"I didn't know you were in the shower!"

"The sound of water running didn't clue you in?"

"I didn't listen at the door. I'm not a pervert."

"Are you saying I'm a pervert?"

"No. I'm saying you should lock the door."

"This is my house. I'm not used to locking the door."

"Well, get used to it!"

I finally make it to the towel. I get to my knees to wrap it around me, but in my rush, I hit my head against the vanity. "Ouch!"

Zane leaps out of the bathtub and hurries to me. "Did you hurt yourself?"

He pushes my hair out of the way to examine my head. I slap his hands away. "I'm fine."

He kneels in front of me and my gaze drops to his chest. The spattering of hair doesn't distract from his muscular build. Wide shoulders, narrow hips, and a six-pack of abs in between. How I'd love to trace every single muscle with my tongue.

He snatches my towel from the floor and opens it. "Here," he says as he covers me with the material.

"Thank you," I murmur as I secure the towel.

"I promise I'll lock the door from now on. I wasn't thinking."

"And I'll make sure there's no one in the shower before I barge inside."

He smiles and two dimples appear on his left cheek. They only add to his sex appeal. As if he needs to be any sexier.

"We have a deal. Do you want to shake on it?"

"Nope. I'm good." No way in hell am I letting go of this towel. With my luck, it'll fall to the ground and it'll appear as if I'm offering myself to Zane as a sacrifice.

I second this idea.

I ignore my inner voice. She's always getting me in trouble.

But I'm fun.

Adele cries before I can give in to temptation. Because, let's face it, I was going to give in. There's a reason why I'm without a home at thirty-one, despite working since I was sixteen after all.

Zane cringes. "Duty calls."

"I can go."

He smiles but his dimples don't make an appearance. "She's my responsibility."

I frown. Adele isn't a responsibility. She's a gift to be treasured.

"Let me know if you need anything."

"I'm good." He stands. "Enjoy your shower."

The second he shuts the door behind him, I slump to the floor. Phew. That was too close for comfort.

I need to keep my hands off Zane Raider. He's a player, and players don't stick around. And I want a man who sticks. Who wants to build a family and a home with me.

Zane Raider is not that man.

Chapter 11

"Apparently, a simple lawyer meeting requires my entire family."

ZANE

My knee bounces up and down as I sit in the lawyer's waiting room.

"You okay?" Eli asks.

"Fine."

He nods at my knee. "Fine?"

"I don't know what I'm doing here," I admit.

He frowns. "You still want to give Adele back to her mom?"

"Yes. No. I don't know." I run a hand through my hair and pull on the ends. The bite of pain doesn't help to calm any of the thoughts whizzing through my brain at breakneck speed.

He places a hand on my thigh to stop my knee from bouncing. "Which is why we're here. In case you decide to keep Adele, you should know your options."

"We don't know Adele's mine. I mean..." I glance around the waiting room to ensure no one can overhear us, but we're the only people here. "I don't remember Daisy."

"Not a flicker of recognition?"

"None. And I'm not exactly father material."

He scowls. "Why not?"

He has to ask? "I didn't grow up with a dad."

His scowl deepens.

"It's different for you. You were sixteen when Dad left. I was eleven."

"Mr. Raider?" the secretary calls. "Follow me."

I stand and push the baby stroller down the hallway as I follow the secretary. She shows me into a small meeting room.

"Have a seat. Ms. Kline will be with you in a moment."

Eli and I sit next to each other but I last less than ten seconds before I spring to my feet and begin pacing around the room. I don't know what I'm doing here. I don't know what I'm doing, period. I'm supposed to be in Argentina by now. Not at a lawyer's office in Smuggler's Rest discussing paternity and custody.

The door opens and a woman I vaguely recognize enters. "Mr. Raider?" she greets.

Eli chuckles. "Mr. Raider? I remember when you used to call him Mr. Poopy Pants."

I growl. "I am not Mr. Poopy Pants."

The woman snorts. "Not anymore."

I study her. I should know who she is. Smuggler's Rest isn't very big, and since I've lived here my entire life, I know most people. Although I do enjoy traveling as often as I can.

"Siena. I was in Jaxon's class."

Phew. This isn't another woman I've slept with and don't remember. I might be a player, but I'm not an asshole.

We shake hands before she settles in a chair on the opposite side of the table. She opens a notebook. "My secretary said this was a paternity matter. I'm surprised you came to me, Eli. Don't you usually use those fancy attorneys in New York when a woman claims you're the father of her child?"

"It's not for me." Eli waves toward me. "Zane's the one with the problem."

I frown. Adele isn't a problem. An inconvenience? Maybe. But a problem? No way. She's an innocent baby.

Siena's eyes widen but she clears her throat and wipes the surprise from her face. "Is this your baby?"

"I don't know."

Her brows lift, but to her credit, she doesn't throw any personal questions my way. "Explain, please."

"A woman dropped her off at my house last week. She claimed I'm the dad and took off."

"And who is this woman?"

"She said her name is Daisy."

"I have my private investigators searching for her," Eli adds.

"And you came to me to make this situation legal?" Kind of? I don't know. Luckily, she doesn't wait for a response before continuing. "Have you done a paternity test yet?"

"I made an appointment for him at the lab," Eli answers.

Siena nods in approval. "Good. Home paternity tests aren't admissible in court."

Admissible in court? Crap. Is this a court matter?

"Once we have the results of the test, we can file for custody."

"File for custody?" I squeak. I clear my throat and try again. "File for custody?"

Siena's brow wrinkles. "It's why you're here, isn't it? To ensure you have custody of your baby?"

"I don't know if she is my baby." My stomach sours. The words feel like a betrayal. It's true, though. I don't know if Adele is mine.

I glance at her sleeping in the stroller. She might not be mine, but I can't abandon her. I'm not an asshole. I refuse to be my dad.

"Don't worry. There is precedent for a person receiving custody without being the biological parent to the child. It'll be a more difficult path to wander, but we'll cross that bridge when we know about the child's paternity."

"Her name is Adele."

The words slip out before I can stop them. I can't help it. Adele isn't 'the baby'. She's Adele. A cranky baby who sleeps all day but never at night. Who has the cutest toothless smile I've ever seen.

The door bursts open and Mom barges inside. Followed by my brothers Kai, Miles, Rhett, and Jaxon.

"I'm sorry," the secretary says as she rushes in after them. "I tried to stop them."

"Stop me?" Mom glares at her. "They're discussing my grandchild. I should be here."

"Perhaps, but why am I here?" Jaxon lifts his glasses to pinch his nose.

Miles elbows him. "We're here to support our brother."

"Couldn't we support him while working?"

Kai rolls his eyes. "You really don't understand how this brother supporting brother thing works, do you?"

"I don't understand how standing behind him while he has a meeting with an attorney is supporting him."

Siena giggles. "Jaxon Raider, you haven't changed a bit since high school."

"Incorrect. I have gained ten pounds, have several university degrees, and I'm married."

"You're married? And I thought the shocking news of the day was Zane having a baby."

Miles barks out a laugh. "How is it shocking that Zane has a baby?"

Mom purses her lips. "Miles Raider, behave."

Miles bats his eyelashes at her. "I am behaving. It's not my fault Zane is a player."

Mom sighs. "Yes, well…"

Silence falls. Uncomfortable silence during which I question every decision I've ever made in my life. Am I the asshole? Should I have been more careful? More discreet?

"Should I get more chairs or ring security?" the receptionist asks.

Siena sighs. "No need for security. Besides, the Raider brothers probably know all the security people on Smuggler's Hideaway anyway."

"Only those who attend Mermaid Karaoke," Miles claims and I groan.

Referring to Mermaid Karaoke – when single women descend on the island in search of love – is not helping me make the case of being an upstanding citizen who can care for a baby.

There I go again. Worrying about Adele's future. Her future isn't my concern to worry about.

"We're good," Rhett claims before pulling out a chair for Mom. "No more chairs needed." He sits in the only other available chair while Jaxon, Miles, and Kai lean against the wall.

The receptionist waits for Siena's nod before exiting the room and shutting the door behind her.

"Now," Mom says. "How are we going to ensure baby Adele stays in the Raider family?"

My heart warms at how fierce Mom's words are. She doesn't know if Adele is mine, but she doesn't care. She's going to include this child in our family no matter what.

How could anyone abandon this woman? She's beautiful, loyal, and funny. But my dad did abandon her. And I carry his genes in me.

"We need to prove she's Zane's child before we can begin."

Mom scoffs at Siena. "Have you seen her eyes? Adele has the Raider blue eyes."

Siena purses her lips. "I'm afraid judges don't accept eye color as proof of paternity."

"What proof do they accept?"

"A paternity test."

Mom looks to me. "When are you doing one?"

"I already scheduled it for tomorrow," Eli answers.

Mom nods. "Okay. That's settled. What next?"

"If Adele is Zane's child, we—"

"When," Mom corrects. "When we prove Adele is Zane's child."

The lawyer sighs. I bet she didn't expect to be confronted by all six of the Raider brothers this morning. It's a good thing Eli's a billionaire or she'd probably run from the room screaming. Although, she's a smuggler. Smugglers are made of stern stuff.

"After we receive the paternity test results, we can begin with filing for custody."

"I assume custody won't be an issue since the mother abandoned her child."

I squeeze Mom's hand. She's a strong woman, but discussing how someone abandoned her child will bring up her own past of dealing with a man abandoning his children.

She pats my hand. "Don't you worry, Zane. We'll figure this all out."

She's going to be mighty disappointed in me if I decide not to fight for custody of Adele. But isn't it better to let her mother raise her, than for her to be raised by a man who shouldn't be a father?

Chapter 12

"Turns out Zane needs diaper lessons. At four in the morning. Lucky me."

Sloane

I collapse on the bed and Boozer immediately snuggles into me. I'm surprised he's not repulsed by how bad I smell. But I refuse to shower at three in the morning. I won't be responsible for waking Adele.

I wrap my arms around Boozer and fall to sleep.

"WAH!"

I groan. Adele has some lungs on her for such a small baby.

"WAH!"

I bury my head under the pillow. Zane is supposed to care for Adele in the middle of the night. Since it's still dark out, he's up.

"WAH!"

And now I'm up.

I crawl out of bed and stumble to the nursery. "What's going on? Why is Adele screaming?"

"It's fine. Go back to bed."

I snort. It's fine are words I learned to ignore when I was eight and Mom decided to bake hash brownies and serve them to the women at the PTA meeting for shits and giggles. It was not fine. Which is why we moved two weeks later.

"What's the problem?" I push the hair out of my face so I can scan the room.

Adele squirms in Zane's arms. Judging by the stain on his shirt, she needs changing.

"You need to change her."

"I know. I'm trying."

I lift an eyebrow. "By holding her in your arms?"

"This shit's hard."

I giggle. "Pun intended?"

He glares at me. "You're not funny."

"I'm a little bit funny." I clear my throat. "But, seriously, how have you not figured out how to change her diaper yet? You've had her for a week now."

His cheeks darken. "Mom's been helping out."

My eyes widen. "You let your mother change all of your daughter's diapers?"

He shrugs. "She had six boys. She's an expert."

I didn't expect to give a baby changing lesson at four a.m., but here we are, and here we go. I point to the changing table. "Lay the baby down."

"She cries when I lay her down."

"She's going to cry until her diaper's changed."

"Fine." He lays her on the table.

"Now, remove her onesie."

He fumbles with the snaps.

"What is the problem? It's a onesie. It's not a NASA space suit."

"She won't stop squirming," he mutters as he finally gets the snaps open.

"Good job. Now open and remove the dirty diaper."

He peels back the diaper and recoils. "How can something this small make something this foul?"

"Ah, the joys of parenthood."

He holds the diaper up in the air.

"Put it in the diaper bucket."

He throws the diaper away and the smell in the room immediately improves. "Ah, this is why my family gave me a diaper bucket."

"You're starting to get it, daddy-o."

He grabs a fresh diaper from the stack, but I stop him. "Hold up. You need to clean her first."

"Clean her?"

I point to the baby wipes. "With those."

He snags one and starts wiping from back to front. I stop him. "Don't ever wipe from back to front unless you want her at the doctor's tomorrow."

He groans. "There are rules? There are rules for poop?"

Adele squirms and kicks the baby wipe container. It crashes to the ground. "You need to distract her before she poops all over you."

His eyes widen. "Poops all over me? It's possible for her to poop all over me?"

"Not only possible but pretty much a given. She'll poop on you. Pee on you. Throw up on you. Think of a body fluid and she'll manage to get it on you."

"How is this my life?" he grumbles.

"Oh no. Do you need me to explain the birds and the bees to you? Can it wait until morning? I need to do some research and maybe buy a book and a puppet."

"Funny girl, I don't need you to explain sex to me."

"Phew. I was worried there for a minute."

Adele kicks and hits Zane in the eye. "Motherfucker."

I wag my finger at him. "No swearing in front of the baby unless you want her first word to be fuck."

I snag a stuffed mermaid from the toys piled on the rocking chair and shake it in front of Adele's face. She giggles and reaches for it. "Who's a pretty baby?"

I elbow Zane. "She's distracted. Get a clean diaper on her."

He digs a diaper out of the package and lays it on top of her.

"It's not a blanket, genius. Lift her legs up, slide it under."

He manages to get the diaper in place. "Good?"

His insecurity is adorable. He's trying. He's trying to care for this little baby who was dropped on his doorstep with no warning. Maybe I should give him more credit. Maybe I shouldn't be so hard on him.

Adele yelps. Zane stuck the tabs to her skin instead of the diaper.

"She's not a Christmas present you're wrapping. Tabs to tabs. Be careful of her skin."

He frowns. "Damnit. I didn't mean to hurt her."

"It's okay." I squeeze his bicep. Oops! Mistake. His bicep is hard. Reminding me of how strong this man is. Of how much he can handle.

Nope. Nope. Nope. I am not developing a crush on Zane Raider. He's sexy and my body longs for him, but he is not the man for me. Player, remember?

"There," he announces and I force thoughts away from all the dirty things I want to do with him. There's a baby in the room, Sloane! A baby!

He starts to lift her from the table but I stop him. "She's not dressed."

"Oh, right." He reaches for the onesie he removed from her.

"It's dirty."

He shakes his head as he grabs a clean onesie from the pile. "No wonder my family thought I needed two thousand of these."

"Your family really stepped up for you."

He grins. "The Raider brothers are always there for each other."

"Must be nice," I mumble.

"What?"

"Nothing." I force a smile. "Get this little poop monster dressed and then everyone can go back to sleep."

He contemplates me for a moment. Please don't ask. Four in the morning, while changing a poopy diaper, is not the time to reveal all of my secrets.

Eventually, he drops his gaze to concentrate on the baby. My shoulders sag in relief. He struggles with the snaps on the onesie. "Does baby Velcro exist?"

"You'll get used to it."

He lifts Adele up and cuddles her close. "How does she smell this good now? After…" He motions to the diaper pail and his nose wrinkles.

I smooth a hand over her head. "Babies smell good."

His lips turn up as he stares down at his daughter. "Nah. Adele smells good. Other babies are immaterial."

Oh boy. Zane smiling at his baby is sexier than anything I've ever seen before. I need to get out of here before I attack him – baby and all.

But before I can escape, he sniffs. "Speaking of smells, why do you smell like a frat party?"

I groan. "Some out-of-towners decided to challenge a few locals to a drinking game."

He chuckles. "I bet they regret challenging smugglers."

"I warned them Smuggler's Hideaway moonshine wasn't the same as moonshine in other places, but they wouldn't listen."

"Do landlubbers ever listen?"

"When Trent yells at them to get out, they usually do."

His brow wrinkles. "Usually? Are there customers who refuse to leave? They don't attack you, do they?"

My heart warms at his concern for me. It's been a long time since someone was concerned for me. I wave away his concern before my heart can get used to the feeling. This is

Zane. He becomes nauseous whenever anyone uses the word relationship.

"It's all fine. We have a baseball bat behind the bar, and Dave claims to know martial arts."

"Dave? The bartender who used to hide in the boys' bathroom at school to avoid gym class knows martial arts?"

"He…" I trail off when a yawn hits me.

Zane nudges me toward the hallway. "Go. Get some sleep. I promise to keep this little terror quiet until the morning."

He says little terror, but the way he's staring at Adele has my heart melting into a puddle of goo on the floor. Puddle of goo? There will be no puddles of goo where Zane is concerned.

I hurry to my bedroom before I do something I regret. Such as fall head over heels in love with the least available man on Smuggler's Hideaway.

Chapter 13

"Jumped out of a plane today. Still not as terrifying as changing diapers at 3 a.m."

Z*ANE*

"You're certain this is okay?" I ask Sloane.

She rolls her eyes. "For the millionth time, get out of here. I've got this."

I know she does. She's the one who taught me how to change a diaper when I realized I couldn't phone my mom every time Adele needed changing.

"Okay. I'll be back before dinner."

She waves me away. "Don't worry about it. I have the night off from *Rumrunner*."

Guilt stabs me in the chest. She works full-time at the bar. She shouldn't be spending her day off babysitting for me.

But this is the deal we made, I remind myself. She gets a place to live for free, and I get a nanny for when I need to escape the island.

"Thanks."

She salutes me. Damn, she's cute and sexy and beyond sweet, holding my baby in her arms.

"Now, go jump out of a plane or go boarding down the side of the mountain or do high jumps with a motorcycle or whatever it is you're going to do."

"Just skydiving today."

"Just skydiving." She scoffs. "Just another boring day at the office."

My days at the office are extremely boring. But I don't complain. If it weren't for Eli, I'd be forced to find a job away from Smuggler's Hideaway and probably have to – gulp – wear a tie. No thanks.

"Go." She shoos me away. "You're going to be late."

Late? I'm never late when it's time to do an extreme sport or catch a flight out of here. But when I check my watch, I notice I am indeed running late.

I kiss Adele's hair. "Bye, baby girl. Behave for Sloane."

I hesitate on the porch and Sloane shoves me. "Go."

I don my helmet as I make my way to my motorcycle. I straddle my bike and glance back one more time at my family. No, not my family. The baby I'm currently caring for and the nanny.

I rev the engine and away I go. I don't look back again.

I arrive at the airfield forty-five minutes later. Unfortunately, there isn't an airfield on Smuggler's Hideaway. The island is too small.

Between the three towns of Smuggler's Rest, Rogue's Land-ing, and Pirate's Perch, as well as the *Mermaid Mystical Gardens* amusement park, *Sirens & Stables* horse stables, *Barnacles & Barnyards* petting zoo, and all the other tourist stops, there isn't any room for an airfield on the small island.

"Hey, man," I'm greeted with back slaps and handshakes by my three buddies – Mac, Layne, and Conner.

"I thought you were motorcycling around South America and wouldn't make it," Mac says.

"Change of plans."

Layne laughs. "There's always a change of plans with you."

I shrug since he isn't wrong. I'm a free spirit. I come and go as I please. Except those days are over now since I'm a dad.

Are they? I don't have to fight Daisy for custody. I can return Adele to her.

Except Eli's private investigator hasn't been able to find Daisy. What kind of mother abandons her baby to a stranger she met for one brief night?

"Come on, straggler." Conner motions me toward the hangar.

I push thoughts of Daisy and Adele out of my head – today is my day to have fun and forget about my worries – and hurry to follow.

The hangar isn't very busy. In the summer, it's packed with tourists making tandem jumps, but it's December now, and only the diehard skydivers – me and my buddies – are here.

I get my parachute out of my storage bin and find a spot. I haven't jumped in a while and want to repack it. I open it up and condoms fly everywhere.

Conner, Layne, and Mac burst into laughter.

"We thought you might need some protection considering recent events," Layne manages to say in between bouts of laughter.

I give him the finger. "You knew why my plans changed all along."

"Dude." Conner shakes his head. "The news traveled across Smuggler's Hideaway faster than a sighting of Sammy."

Sammy's a seal that lives on the island. He was captured by the sea life sanctuary north of the island when he was injured as a pup. After he recuperated, they set him free in the ocean. He didn't make it far before he decided he preferred to stay on land where people feed him.

"You don't live on Smuggler's Hideaway." None of them do.

Conner waggles his eyebrows. "But Serena does."

"Who's Serena?"

"His latest sidepiece," Layne explains.

Sidepiece? Conner's married. Happily married as far as I know.

"What happened to Jenny?" His wife.

"Nothing." Conner shrugs. "She works all the time and doesn't have time for me."

My brow wrinkles. It's Sunday. If he doesn't see his wife enough, he should be home with her and not fooling around with his friends.

Mac groans. "If I have to hear Conner whine one more time about his wife, I'm going to hurl."

"I don't whine," Conner claims.

"Whine. Whine. Whine," Mac teases.

Layne steps between the two. "Enough. The pilot should be here any minute. I want to get at least three jumps in today."

I motion to the concrete floor covered in every color of condom in existence. "Someone needs to pick up all these condoms."

Layne slaps my shoulder. "Get to work."

I find a broom and sweep the condoms into a pile. I nearly throw them away. I don't have time for random sex since I now have Adele.

But I won't always have Adele. My stomach cramps but I ignore it. It's true. I won't always have my baby girl. Her mom will return and my life will go back to normal.

I gather the condoms in a trash bag and throw it into my locker.

"Here." Layne hands me a beer as I get to work on packing my parachute.

"I'm good."

"You're not going to change now that you're a dad, are you?" He motions to Mac. "He hasn't changed since his kids came around."

I don't want to discuss this topic and the easiest way to avoid it? Accept the beer. Which I do.

He pats my back and I return to my parachute. I don't need more than five minutes to pack it, considering I've been jumping since I was eighteen years old and saved enough money from my job at *Wok the Plank* to pay for skydiving lessons.

The pilot arrives and I don my wing suit before hitching my parachute on my back. I follow Mac into the airplane while Conner talks on the phone and Layne has another beer.

I frown. Two beers before noon is a bit excessive. Has he always drunk this much?

"How you doing with this dad gig?" Mac asks once we're seated on the bench inside the plane.

"I don't know how you do it, man. The midnight feedings, the dirty diapers, the crying. Fuck. The crying about does me in."

He shrugs. "It's easy. I visit my kids once a month. No worries about all the other crap."

Once a month? I can't imagine spending only one day a month with Adele. But if Daisy has custody, I'll be lucky if I see her once a month.

My stomach falls to the floor. I don't want to be an absent dad. I don't want my kid to grow up wondering what he did wrong. Why he wasn't enough for his dad to stay.

And I don't want to miss out on Adele growing up. She's already changed so much in the week I've lived with her. I can't imagine missing her first words, her first steps, her first day of school.

I'm falling in love with my daughter.

The knowledge hits me with such vehemence, I nearly slam my head into the side of the airplane. I contemplate the door. The urge to jump to my feet and hurry back home to Adele – who's starting to mean the world to me – is strong.

Layne and Conner climb into the plane and my chance to escape disappears when they shut the door behind them.

The pilot switches on the engines and a hum of excitement flows through me. I've missed this. Not merely the skydiving. I've missed all of my adventures. My weekends are usually full with skydiving, motocross, or travel.

It isn't long before the pilot indicates it's nearly time to jump. We stand in line at the door to wait for his signal.

The second he gives it, the door is open and Conner jumps first. Followed by Layne. I'm third with Mac bringing up the rear.

I scream into the wind as my heart pumps and adrenaline fills my veins. I wish Adele could see me now. I wonder how old a child needs to be before they can make a tandem jump. I'll find out. If Adele is mine, she'll enjoy skydiving as much as I do.

I'm busy contemplating my baby and nearly miss the cues for our formation. We practice building a few shapes before it's time to open our parachutes and land.

We do two more jumps before I decide to pack it in.

"What are you doing?" Conner asks when I open my locker to put away my parachute. "We have time for another jump."

"Sorry, I need to get home."

"At least have another beer with us before you go," Layne insists.

I hold up my hands. "No more beer. I'm on my bike."

"You've had two beers. You're fine."

I am fine. But if I have another beer, I won't be.

"No worries," Conner says. "We can have a beer on the island. Did I tell you Serena has a best friend who's single?" He waggles his eyebrows. "I love threesomes."

I have no interest in Serena's friend and he shouldn't either. He's married. I'm not usually the moral police, but I watched Mom fall apart when she found out Dad left her for another woman. I could never cause that pain.

Mac slaps me on the shoulder. "Once you get the custody arranged, you'll have more time to spend with us."

Except I don't want to give up custody of Adele. I want my daughter in my life every day. Not one day a month. The thought still shocks me, but it feels right.

I stalk to my bike, wondering if my friends have always been this big of assholes. How did I miss this? A cheater, a drinker, and a negligent father.

If this is my normal life, I need a new normal. Maybe a new normal, including a baby girl named Adele and her sexy nanny.

Slow your boat, Zane. Adele is my baby and I shouldn't abandon her but Sloane is a step too far. Relationships are not for me.

Except...

Being a dad wasn't for me either.

Chapter 14

"Nothing good ever follows the words 'Aren't you going to let me in?'"

SLOANE

I yawn as I make my way from the bedroom to the kitchen. I should still be in bed, but Zane has a meeting this morning and asked me to watch Adele earlier than usual.

I couldn't say no. Saying no to Zane is difficult enough, but when he's holding an adorable baby in his arms? It's impossible.

I really need to save some money and find a place to stay that doesn't include temptation on a daily basis.

"Good morning," he greets when I enter the kitchen.

I grunt. I'm not usually a morning person and today I've had even less sleep than usual.

He hands me a cup of coffee. "Milk and no sugar. The way you drink it."

My eyes widen. Zane knows how I drink my coffee? Nope. I'm not going to read anything into this. He doesn't care for me. He is simply observant.

"Thanks," I mutter before taking a cautious sip. It's perfect. Enough milk to kill the bitter taste, but not too much to make the coffee milky.

The doorbell rings. I sigh before setting my coffee down. "I'll get it."

"If it's one of my brothers, don't let them in. They'll hide some kind of prank and we won't find it until the smell gets to us."

I giggle, but when I open the door and see who's standing on the porch, the giggle dies in my throat. This isn't one of his brothers. Not even close.

Mom flips her dyed blonde hair over her shoulder. "Aren't you going to let me in?"

I open the door and motion her inside.

"What are you doing here?"

She snorts. "What am I doing here? What are *you* doing here?"

"I live here." My brow wrinkles. "Speaking of which, how do you know where I live?"

It's not as if she keeps in touch. Unless showing up every few months for money is considered keeping in touch. Not in my book, it isn't.

"Some woman at your former apartment building told me where you're living."

I groan. I'm going to kill Melanie. I'll poison her moonshine. No one will figure out it was me.

It's bad enough, she had me kicked out of my home. She couldn't send Mom on a wild goose chase? It's what Smugglers usually do with visitors who aren't tourists.

"What do you want?"

She plants a hand on her hip and her bangles clink with the movement. The bangles are part of her whole hippie outfit. The hippie movement died in the early 70s – when my mom was still a toddler – but she clings to the movement as if it were her own invention.

She's wearing a loose, flowing top in tie-dye. She paired it with a long, white skirt. And, since it's December and chilly, she topped the outfit with a fringe jacket. She hasn't changed a bit.

"Is that any way to treat your mother?"

I bark out a laugh. "Mother? Some kind of mother you were."

"I birthed you."

"Which is pretty much when you stopped being a mother."

She rolls her eyes. "You always were such a dramatic child."

"I was a dramatic child because I wanted dinner, but we couldn't afford it because you'd spent all your money on booze and marijuana?"

She sighs. "I don't know what your problem is with marijuana. It's perfectly legal."

I throw my hands in the air. "I don't give a shit if marijuana was legal. I was hungry and wanted dinner."

She dismisses me with a flick of her hand, causing those damn bangles to jingle again. I swear she cares more about those bangles than she does me.

"You got breakfast and lunch at school."

"In case you missed the memo, there are three meals in a day."

She definitely missed the memo. Mom is skinny as a rail. Probably because she continues to spend all of her money on booze and marijuana.

For the record, I don't have a problem with either one of those substances. I'm a bartender on Smuggler's Hideaway for mermaid's sake! But when you don't have money left over to feed your kid? That I have a problem with.

Zane strolls into the living room carrying Adele in his arms. My face heats. The last person in the entire world I want to witness this interaction is him.

Mom's gaze rakes up and down Zane. I fight the urge to stand in front of him to protect him from her. Mom doesn't have an issue with age. Young, old, extremely old? It doesn't matter to her.

"Who's this?" She actually licks her lips. Licks her lips.

"This is Zane, and the baby is Adele."

"Baby?" Her lips purse. Did she not notice Adele on Zane's hip? She's hard to miss. "Do you have a baby?"

I open my mouth to correct her but she carries on without listening to me – nothing new there. "I thought I taught you better. Children will weigh you down. You're better off without one."

"I'm well aware of how you feel children will weigh you down."

"Don't get snarky with me, young woman."

My nostrils flare as anger fills me. How dare she boss me around! "You literally told me less than a minute ago how I weighed you down and you would have been better off without me. I'm pretty sure I'm entitled to be snarky."

"You always were such a righteous child." She motions to Zane and Adele. "And now here you are with a husband and child. I am disappointed in you."

It's a good thing I no longer care if she's disappointed in me. Otherwise, those words would wound worse than a jellyfish sting. And everyone knows jellyfish stings are the worst.

Zane clears his throat. "Mrs. Wilder—"

"It's Poppy, darling. I'm not married. Never have been." She bats her eyelashes and bites her bottom lip.

She believes Zane is my husband, and she's still hitting on him. Now do you understand why I'm not worried about getting my mother's approval?

He steps closer to me and places a hand on my hip. "How can we help you today?"

She sighs at the hand on my hip. "At least you found a faithful man. Most men aren't, you know."

Yes, I know. My father wasn't faithful. He was a player who played Mom when she was young. He got her pregnant and then disappeared. I've never met him. I don't even know his name. Assuming 'that man' isn't a proper name.

Zane squeezes my hip before releasing me. "Sloane and I aren't together."

"Oh." Mom's eyes light with interest. "You have an open relationship? Perfect."

I stare at the floor. If ever there was a time for a hole to open up and swallow me whole, now is the moment. I wait but nothing happens. Darn it.

"I'm his nanny," I explain.

"Nanny?" Her nose wrinkles. "You choose to be involved with a child when it's not required? How odd."

"Ms. Wilder." Zane waits until her attention is on him. "I think it's time for you to leave."

She doesn't make a move toward the door. Of course not. Far be it for my mother to listen to anyone but herself. "But I haven't had a chance to catch up with my daughter yet."

Catch up? What an odd way of saying beg for money.

"She doesn't appear to want to catch up with you."

"It's her face. I believe the young people refer to it as 'resting bitch face'."

Zane growls. "Tell me I misheard. You did not just say your daughter has resting bitch face."

Mom clutches her chest. "I'm sorry. Did I use the term wrong?"

She knows exactly how to use the term. But is she fooling Zane with this innocent act? I glance over at him. His jaw clenches, and a muscle in his cheek pulses. He's not fooled.

I knew there was a reason I liked Zane. As a person. Not as a potential partner. Unlike my mother, I don't fling myself at every available and some non-available men.

"I'm trying to ask you politely to leave. But I can forget the polite."

"To leave?" She blinks. "You want me to leave?"

Despite evidence to the contrary, she's not deaf. She heard Zane when he told her it's time for her to leave. But she only hears what she wants to. And I'm the one who's stubborn.

"I want you to leave and to stop harassing your daughter."

Warmth fills me until my knees wobble. No one's ever stood up for me with Mom before.

Not the school guidance counselors, not the police officers who responded to the emergency call when she started a fire by putting her shoes in the oven, not the neighbors who mooched liquor from her, and definitely not the boyfriends who leered at me and made me feel uncomfortable.

"You can't harass your own daughter," Mom argues instead of leaving the way she was asked.

"Enough."

Zane hands me Adele and the little girl immediately curls into me. She knows she's safe with me. She'll always be safe with me. No matter what my relationship with Zane is, this little girl will never be harmed. Not if I can help it.

"Ms. Wilder." He motions toward the door.

When Mom doesn't move, he herds her toward the door without touching her. It's impressive.

He opens the door and ushers her out. She stands on the porch and sputters nonsense at him but he shuts the door in her face.

I want to clap. It would be bad manners to clap or?

I also want to throw myself at Zane and thank him with my tongue for his help.

Whoa, Sloane. No thanking the player with your tongue. It would be entirely too easy to fall for this man who showed me a caring side of himself I've never seen before.

Hands – and tongue – off!

Chapter 15

"Nothing like a crying baby to ruin your timing."

ZANE

I stare at the door I closed on Sloane's mother. What a bitch! How dare she treat her daughter this way!

Anger courses through me. Parents should love and protect their children. Not treat them as cheap toys to be discarded when they're no longer fun or useful.

I inhale a deep breath and force my muscles to relax. I am not taking my anger out on Sloane. Something tells me she's had enough of people taking their anger out on her.

"Zane?"

I hate how small and uncertain Sloane's voice sounds.

"Sorry," I say as I turn around and approach her. "Let me put Adele down and then we'll talk."

Her eyes widen. "Talk?"

I settle my baby girl on my hip before kissing Sloane's cheek. "Talk."

I place Adele in her crib and wait to make certain she's settled. Once it's clear she's asleep, I nab the baby monitor and tiptoe out of the room.

I half expect Sloane to be hiding in her bedroom, but when I reach the living room, she's sitting on the couch with Boozer's head in her lap. She scratches behind his ears as she stares outside.

I clear my throat. "Ahem."

When she doesn't respond, I try again. Also, unsuccessful.

I kneel in front of her and grasp her hands. "Come back to me, Sloane."

She startles. "Oh, hey."

I grin. "Where did you go?"

She shrugs. "Just thinking."

"Does she always act this way?"

She widens her eyes and blinks a few times. Great. She's going to pretend she doesn't know what I'm talking about. I lift a brow and she sighs. All signs of rebellion leave her.

"Yeah."

"What about your dad?"

"My dad?"

I squeeze her hands. "Your dad."

She scowls. "I don't know who he is."

"What?"

"Mom never told me who he was. The only thing she ever said was he's a player who dumped her when she got pregnant."

Things are beginning to make sense now. No wonder Sloane always makes nasty comments about me. She's lumped me together with her dad.

But I'm not the same as him. I didn't run away when Daisy dumped Adele on my doorstep. I considered it a few times, but I didn't do it. And there's no way I'm letting my baby girl go now. She's captured my heart. She's mine.

"Your mom raised you alone?"

She snorts. "Raised? If you consider forgetting to feed me or refusing to buy me school supplies or moving from state to state, raising me, I guess she raised me."

No wonder Sloane's flaky. Her mom never taught her any better. Her mom never taught her anything. Except, how to be unreliable and unpredictable. I'll cut her some slack the next time she's late.

"I'm sorry for what you went through."

She wrenches her hands from mine. "Do not pity me. I don't need your pity."

I raise my hands in the air. "I don't pity you. I commiserate with you."

"What do you know about it?" She snarls. "You with your perfect family. Your loving mother, your five brothers who would literally stand in front of a moving truck for you."

I hold up a finger. "Technically, it was a car, not a truck."

"This isn't funny." She leaps to her feet and Boozer yelps. She starts pacing around the living room. "I don't have five brothers who rush to help me whenever life slaps me down. There's no one to buy me an entire room of baby stuff because I found out I'm a dad. There's no mom to change my baby's diaper, so I don't have to."

I stand and cross my arms over my chest. "I might have had five brothers, but I didn't have a dad. He left when I was eleven."

She screeches to a halt. "Your mom is divorced?"

"Divorced is a nice way of saying my dad abandoned us right before Eli's sixteenth birthday and no one's seen or heard from him since."

"He doesn't pay child support?"

"He hasn't had a thing to do with us since he began his new family."

Her eyes widen. "His new family?"

"And now you know why I can't be a good dad." The words slip out but I don't regret them. It's a relief to actually say the words out loud.

"Hold on. You think you can't be a good dad because your dad abandoned you?"

"I didn't have a good dad growing up. How would I know how to be one?"

"I might not have realized your dad left when you were young, but I do know you had great role models growing up."

"Role models?"

She rolls her eyes. "Your brothers. Eli and Rhett. Those two would do anything for you."

"It's not the same."

"Maybe not. But they were there for you. They showed you how to be a good man. And your mom would literally burn down the entire island for you." She grasps my hands. "You know how to be a dad, Zane. Let me rephrase, you are a good dad."

"I mess up all the time. You had to teach me how to change a diaper."

"Have you ever left Adele crying in her crib?"

I rear back. "Of course not."

"Have you ever not changed her diaper even though you didn't know what you were doing?"

"I'm not letting her lay in her own filth."

She smiles. "There you have it. You're a good dad." Her smile fades. "Trust me. I know. Because you're doing the exact opposite of what my mom would do." The sparkle in her dark brown eyes fades. "My mom would have left me on the porch if someone had abandoned me there."

I place a hand on her cheek. "I'm sorry."

"Don't be. I'm used to it."

"It still has to hurt."

She shrugs. "It sucks not having anyone during the holidays when everyone else is spending time with their families, but it's not so bad. I get the best seats at the cinema."

My heart breaks for her. She doesn't have any family to spend the holidays with? Did she spend Thanksgiving alone?

She won't be spending Christmas alone. Or any other holidays for that matter. Whether she's my nanny or not, she's welcome at the Raider table for the holidays.

"You're spending Christmas with my family."

"You can't decide I'm spending the holiday with your family."

"I can and I did."

"I won't be your charity case."

"Who said anything about charity?"

"You're inviting me to spend Christmas with you because you feel sorry for me."

I growl. "I do not feel sorry for you."

"Yeah, right."

I palm her neck and pull her near. "I never knew how strong you were."

"You've seen me lift a keg at the bar before."

"Not what I meant, and you know it. You, Sloane Wilder, are one of the strongest people I know."

Tears form in her eyes but she blinks them away. "Thank you, Zane Raider."

"I want to kiss you."

She looks up at me from beneath her eyelashes. "I won't stop you."

I don't hesitate. I crush my lips to hers. She wraps her arms around my waist and presses her chest to mine. I moan at the feel of her hard nipples. I want to strip her bare and feel her nipples against my naked chest.

I've wanted Sloane for a long time. Ever since the first time she kicked me out of *Rumrunner*. But she's avoided me when she wasn't snarling at me. Turns out her dislike had nothing to do with me. She looked at me and saw her dad. No more. Now, she'll see me.

"Let me in," I demand.

She opens on a sigh and I thrust my tongue into her mouth. She tastes of mint and coffee. Underneath those tastes is sweet. Pure sweetness. I groan. I've always loved sweet things.

As I explore her mouth with my tongue, she rubs up against me. My cock hardens and lengthens at the feel of this soft woman pressing against it.

Bedroom. We should move this to my bedroom.

I dig my fingers into her hips and she immediately hops up and wraps her legs around my waist. Now her hot center is aligned with my hard cock. Perfect.

I begin walking toward my bedroom with her in my arms. I don't stop kissing her. I can't. Her sweet taste is addicting. Better than the most delicate treat from *Pirate's Pastries.*

"Wah."

Not now, baby girl. Go back to sleep.

"Wah!"

I wrench my lips from Sloane's and rest my forehead against hers. "Sorry, I need to deal with Adele."

Her eyes flutter open. They're full of heat and passion. But then she scans the area and remembers where we are, who I am, and all hints of heat disappear.

She hops down. "It's… I'm…" She doesn't finish her thought before racing away.

I drop my chin to my chest. Shit. She regrets our kiss.

"WAH!"

At least one female in my life wants me.

Chapter 16

*"Serving drinks to the troublemakers instead of being
the troublemaker. Growth, baby."*

SLOANE

"Come on, Boozer." I clap my hands to get his attention.
The big lug sprints to the sea instead of toward me.

I glance at the time on my phone. I guess I can be a few
minutes late to work.

No, you can't, Sloane. Do you want to become your mother?

The thought has me shouting Boozer's name with such
urgency, he instantly returns to me.

"I need to be on time to work," I explain as I hook up his
leash and lead him off the beach toward Zane's house.

"In fact, I should probably buy a watch and start paying
attention to the time."

I do have some money saved since I didn't have to pay rent
this month. I was planning to use the money to buy a ticket for
Mermaid Mystical Gardens. The amusement park is always super
fun and in the holiday season, it's even better. They decorate

the entire park with Christmas trees in mermaid and smuggler themes.

They also charge extra this time of year. But spending my money on an amusement park instead of buying a reliable watch is exactly the sort of thing Mom would do.

I claim to hate how Mom 'raised' me. So, why am I emulating all the things she did? This needs to stop.

Watch it is.

When I arrive at *Rumrunner,* there's no need to rush inside. Or come up with an excuse for being late. Or do my hair as I scurry into the bar.

Huh. Maybe this being on time gig isn't too bad.

"Hi, Harper," I greet my boss, who happens to own the bar. She's also in love with Zane's brother, Kai. They live together with her father.

"How are you doing?"

The sympathetic look on her face has me pausing. "What do you mean?"

"Living with Zane." Her nose wrinkles in disgust.

"Actually, Zane isn't too bad."

She lifts her brows. "The player isn't too bad?"

She knows how I feel about players. She doesn't know the reason why, but she's seen me reject man after man while calling them players ever since I started working at the speakeasy.

I shrug. "He hasn't been fooling around with anyone since I moved in."

Except for me. My body warms as thoughts of our kiss bombard me. I've kissed a lot of men, but never has a single kiss from a man had me wrapping my legs around him while rubbing up against him like a cat in heat.

But this is Zane. The man I've lusted after for years. Lusted after and knew I couldn't have.

Although, maybe I can have him. Zane's changed his opinion on having children in the past weeks. Maybe he's changed his opinion on relationships, too?

I shake my head. I'm doing it again. Acting like my mother. Hoping to change a man when I know better. Men don't change for women.

"He probably doesn't have time," Harper says and I return my attention to her. "I know how much time caring for another person takes."

"How is your father?" She cares for her father, who had a stroke some years ago and is not fully mobile.

"Probably up to something with Kai. Those two are always up to no good." She's complaining, but guessing by the grin on her face, she's happy they have each other.

"Speaking of my father, I have a doctor's appointment with him today. Can you open up?"

"Sure!" I clear my throat and tone down my enthusiasm. "Of course."

She meets my gaze. "Try not to get caught in the walk-in cooler this time."

"I won't. Girl Scout promise." I hold up two fingers.

She shakes her head. "You were never a Girl Scout."

I scowl. "I could have been." If I'd ever lived somewhere for longer than a year at a time.

"I need to go." She starts for the back door. "By the way, I haven't done the riddle for today yet."

"Not a problem."

Rumrunner is a speakeasy. The locals know where it is and can enter without a password, but visitors and tourists have to solve a riddle to enter. There's a new riddle every day.

I skip through the bar to Trent. As the bouncer, he's in charge of ensuring all visitors know the password.

"I have the riddle for you."

"From Harper?"

"Nope. This one's all mine." I already have a riddle made up. I've been waiting for Harper to give me the chance to use it.

"I have no legs, yet I dance in the deep. I sing sailors to ruin, and rock them to sleep. Who am I?"

He rolls his eyes. "Too easy. A mermaid."

"Harper said it had to be easy enough for tourists to solve."

"Mission accomplished."

I giggle and slap his shoulder. "Be nice. Harper's trusting me."

"You got this, girl."

I nod to him before rushing off to do the zillion tasks I need to finish before we can open the bar. By the time the first customer arrives, my bangs are sweaty and clinging to my forehead.

"Here comes trouble," Dave mutters when five women enter the bar.

Trouble is right. Sophia, Chloe, Nova, Maya, and Paisley are the owners of the local brewery, *Five Fathoms.* They're also the reason I got detention for five days my senior year of high school. No senior skip day for me.

I make my way to their table. "No bar fights tonight or I'm kicking you out."

Sophia snorts. "You'd never kick us out."

"Try me."

Paisley studies me. "Living with Zane is improving you. Good."

Chloe, Nova, Maya, and Sophia clap.

"Tell us more!" Chloe insists.

"I don't live with Zane. I'm his nanny for now."

She waggles her eyebrows. "Nanny or *nanny*?"

"I've read this book. The single dad always ends up with the nanny." Maya leans closer. "Have you kissed already?"

I try to fight it, but I can feel the heat spreading on my cheeks.

"She has!" Maya squeals. "I am loving this."

I make a cutting motion across my neck. "Knock it off. I'm not falling in love with a Raider brother. I know better."

Paisley purses her lips. "I'm in love with a Raider. Are you saying I'm an idiot?"

"You're with Eli. He doesn't count."

"I know for a fact his last name is Raider. He's reminded me enough times when he's needling me to change my name upon marriage."

I latch onto the change of subject. "Is that why you're not married yet? You don't want to change your name, but he wants you to?"

She wags her finger at me. "Nuh uh. We are not changing the topic away from you kissing Zane."

"I never said I kissed Zane."

"But your face did," Nova claims.

See what I mean? These five are trouble to their cores. It doesn't matter how they've all found love and settled down. They're still shit stirrers. It's a good thing only one of them is with a Raider. The world would implode if all five of them were with the five Raider brothers.

"Let's get champagne to celebrate," Maya says.

"Champagne?" Sophia's nose wrinkles. "We don't celebrate with champagne on Smuggler's Hideaway."

Maya sighs. "I was hoping to survive our night out without having the worst hangover in the world tomorrow."

"You can't claim to always have the worst hangover in the world after a night out. By definition, worst only occurs once." Paisley is such a nerd.

"Shots it is!" Chloe declares. She's a wild child. Getting married and having a twelve-year-old step-daughter hasn't changed her one bit.

I shake my head. "I still can't believe you married a cop."

"He's sexy and knows how to use handcuffs. What's not to love?"

"Plus, he won't throw her crazy ass in jail," Sophia adds.

While they argue about the comfort of the Smuggler's Hideaway jail cells, I return to the bar for a bottle of moonshine and some shot glasses.

Dave moans. "It's going to be one of those kinds of nights."

"Not my fault the crazy five are here."

I set the bottle of moonshine on their table and hand out shot glasses.

"You're missing a glass," Sophia says.

"You need to drink a shot with us," Chloe adds.

"Nope. I'm holding down the fort today since Harper is dealing with her dad."

"I like this version of you," Paisley says.

I roll my eyes. "I'm pretty sure you liked the version of me who ended up getting detention because I took the blame for the 'locker room' incident."

"Sorry," Nova says but she doesn't appear the least bit sorry. "I couldn't get caught setting fire to yet another one of Hudson's girlfriends' lockers."

"Let me guess. Your husband still doesn't know what you did."

Nova and Hudson got together when she wound up pregnant after they ended up locked together in a chalet overnight at his resort.

She smirks. "Oh, he knows. And I've been properly punished. Trust me."

Sophia lifts her glass in the air. "Here's to the bootleggers. Masters of the sneaky snip and secret stashes. Thanks for keeping the party alive."

"To the bootleggers!" The rest shout before downing their shots.

"Have fun and behave," I order as I leave them.

"Whoever thought Sloane would tell anyone to behave?" Chloe hollers after me.

I ignore her. Chloe was dubbed the wild child by the entire island. She can't throw stones at me.

Besides, I'm changing. I'm not going to be the flaky woman no one could depend on before. My days of acting like my mom are over.

Chapter 17

"Biggest news of my life and all I got was dog snacks and moonshine."

ZANE

My phone beeps with a message as I park in the driveway of Eli's house. House? Mansion is a more accurate description. It fits since he's a billionaire.

I wish my college roommate was a genius who invented silly apps that earned billions. Instead, my college roommate was an extreme sports fanatic who got me hooked on Parkour.

Although, I quit competing when I broke my ankle in Greece. I was perfectly fine to continue, but Mom lost her mind when I phoned her from the hospital on Santorini.

I learned my lesson. Do not tell Mom what I'm doing. She can know where I am but not what I'm up to. It's better this way. She still thinks skydiving is dangerous.

I dig my phone out of my pocket to respond to the message. Except it's not a message, it's an email. From the lab where I took my paternity test.

My heart races as I stare at the notification. What if Adele isn't mine? What then?

I'd have to let her go. To return her to her mom.

My stomach clenches at the thought of returning Adele to the woman who abandoned her. What kind of person abandons their child? It doesn't matter. I'm not letting Daisy raise Adele.

Adele has captured my heart. I am not letting her go. Paternity be damned. She is mine.

I open the email and scan it. *Statement of results. The genetic markers strongly support the conclusion that the tested male is the biological father. Probability of paternity. 99.9%. Indicates a high probability of paternity, with a conclusive result.*

I drop the phone in my lap and rock back in my seat. Adele is mine. She's my daughter. My baby girl. I don't have to give her up.

I can't wait to tell Sloane. She believes in me. Believes I can be a good father.

But she's at work and my brothers are waiting on me. I climb out of the car and start for the door but then I remember my good luck charm.

It's the Raider brothers' monthly poker night and a good luck charm is required. Eli has a set of teeth he used to scare us with when we were young. Rhett has a bowling shoe, which is weird, but whatever. Jaxon has a Chia pet he claims resembles Elvis. It doesn't.

Miles has a rabbit's foot that definitely is not from a rabbit. And Kai has a pickle in the jar he calls Mr. Crisp.

I'm the only one with a 'normal' good luck charm. I snatch the taxidermized squirrel in a cowboy hat from the front seat before heading for Eli's house.

"Someone's happy tonight," Kai says when I enter the house.

"He must think he's going to win." Miles snorts. "Delusional."

"Or he's happy because he kissed Sloane," Eli says.

Rhett rubs his hands together. "Pay up, suckers."

Jaxon pushes his glasses up his nose. "I didn't bet against Sloane and Zane getting together. I wouldn't bet against Zane. He's been staring at her with lust in his eyes for years."

I can't deny it. Sloane is the most beautiful woman on Smuggler's Hideaway. Naturally, I've been lusting after her. I'm only a man.

But Sloane isn't the reason I'm smiling. And I'm not discussing my relationship with her with my brothers anyway.

Hold on. I don't have a relationship with Sloane. She's my nanny.

And we kissed. We would have done a lot more if Adele hadn't interrupted.

Adele! She's the reason I'm happy.

"I got the paternity results back." I rock back on my heels.

"And? Is Adele yours?" Eli asks.

Rhett scowls. "I don't care if she is your daughter biologically. She's your daughter. End of."

Rhett would say that. He adopted two children since Dakota has health issues and was wary of bearing children herself. Plus, she was in the foster system. She wanted to foster children.

Instead, they ended up adopting the first two children they fostered.

"Dude," Miles grumbles. "Don't keep us in suspense."

I can't hold it in anymore. My smile stretches from ear to ear. "Adele is mine."

"Whoo hoo!" My brothers converge on me with back slaps and half hugs.

"This calls for a celebration." Eli lifts a bottle. "Good whiskey?" He lifts another bottle. "Or moonshine?"

"You have to ask?" I hand out shot glasses and he pours moonshine into them.

"Here's to Zane and his little girl, Adele. May her and her cousins, Pearl, Mira, and Stephanie, learn to support each other."

"After they wreak havoc on the Smuggler's Hideaway school system," I add.

"Here! Here!"

"Let's play some poker!" Miles shouts.

We make our way down the hallway to Eli's game room. This room – with its dark green walls and oak paneling – could be in a magazine. On one side of the room is a bar stocked with all the best whiskey and beer Smuggler's Hideaway has to offer. On the other side is the largest television I've ever seen in a private home. There are leather couches scattered around the room so you can sit and enjoy a game while drinking your whiskey.

In the middle of the room is a pool table and a poker table. We sit around the poker table.

Jaxon clears his throat. "I'm allowed to make a new rule each month."

Miles groans. "We know."

Eli and Rhett insisted on this 'rule' because Jaxon felt left out of our prank wars. Until he married Blossom, he refused to participate in them. But his wife is super competitive – even with the prank wars! – and he can't be feeling left out anymore. Nonetheless, the rule continues.

"How's this for a rule? Whenever Zane mentions the baby, he has to drink a shot."

I groan. "No fair. I just found out Adele is my baby."

Kai slams a bottle down next to me. "Is that one or two shots?"

I glare at him as I pour a shot and down it. "Happy?"

"Not yet, but I will be soon."

Rhett rubs his hands together. "Who's ready for some poker?"

He removes the plastic from the deck of cards. Considering the pranks we play on each other and how often we've been known to 'cheat', we use a brand-new deck of cards each month.

Rhett starts to deal the cards, but stops. "What the hell? Why are the cards sticking together? This is a new deck."

Kai bursts into laughter. "It is a new deck."

Rhett smells his hands and cringes. "A new deck covered in maple syrup?"

"I wouldn't say covered."

Miles raises his hand and high-fives Kai. "Good one."

Kai grins. "If anyone's keeping score, I'm winning the prank war."

I roll my eyes. "I don't have time for pranks, I have a baby to care for."

"Drink!" Kai points to the bottle of moonshine.

Shit. At this rate, I'm going to be drunk before the first round of poker is finished.

Poker is serious business in the Raider family. You can't skip a month. Even when Eli lived in California, he flew home for poker night. And the winner has bragging rights for an entire month. Whereas the loser won't hear the end of it until the next poker night.

All this to say – I can't be drunk off my face during poker.

Rhett throws the sticky cards on the table. It's all jokers and queens. I don't know where Kai is getting these novelty cards but someone needs to curtail his online shopping.

"I'll get another deck." Eli makes his way to the bar and unlocks a drawer.

"Do you seriously lock up your cards?" Jaxon asks.

Kai smirks. "I'm extremely proud of myself right now."

"Where are the snacks?" Miles glances around before standing up. "I'll grab them."

Good. I need some food to soak up the shots. I also need to stop talking about Adele. But how am I supposed to stop talking about my baby girl? The baby girl who is without a doubt mine.

Kai points to me. "He's got the goofy grin on his face again."

"He must be thinking about Adele," Jaxon says.

"Or Sloane." Rhett wiggles his eyebrows.

"I guess this means you want to go ahead and sue for custody of Adele," Eli says.

"This isn't fair!" I slap a hand on the table. "Everyone else can speak of…" I cut myself off before I say Adele. "of a certain subject. Why can't I?"

Jaxon fiddles with his glasses. "Because it's funnier this way?"

"I didn't know you were this cruel."

"Maybe you should have shown up at the distillery the day you invited all of those people from the press for a tour."

I cringe. "It wasn't my fault. My flight was cancelled."

"You flew to Iceland for a weekend. Even you should have realized the chance of getting back on time was minimal."

"Ugh. What is it? Pick on Zane day?"

"Yep. It was my idea."

I launch myself at Kai but Rhett pushes his way in between us before I can get my first punch in.

Kai chuckles. "Now you know how it feels to be the brother being made fun of for falling in love."

"I'm not falling in love. I have a new daughter."

"Drink!" My brothers yell in unison.

The moonshine doesn't burn as I drink the shot. This is a bad sign. Smuggler's Hideaway moonshine causes a trail of fire in your esophagus and burns your nose hairs. When it stops burning, you're in trouble.

Miles strolls into the room carrying several large bowls of snacks. "What did I miss?"

"Our brothers are assholes," I grumble as I grab a handful of snacks. I toss the pretzels in my mouth.

Miles bursts into laughter. "How are you enjoying those snacks, bro?"

I frown. "Kind of tough to chew."

"Because they're dog snacks."

I spit them out to lunge at Miles but he dashes off. I give chase.

"Why aren't you stopping him, Rhett?" he asks from where he's hiding behind the bar.

"Dog snacks?" Rhett snorts. "You deserve a beat down."

I launch myself over the bar. Miles covers his face. "Not the face. I need the face to charm women."

"Oh, please. The only woman you want to charm is Hazel and she won't give you the time of day."

"Sloane won't give you the time of day either."

Wrong. Sloane melted into my arms the second I pressed my lips to hers. Considering her father, it'll take work to break down her defenses. Good thing she's living in my house. I have plenty of time to work on tearing down those defenses.

But first, I need to smack my brother upside the head.

Chapter 18

"I can add 'wrangling drunk Raiders' to my resume."

SLOANE

I sigh as I plop down on the sofa in Zane's living room. Boozer jumps up to lay next to me.

Harper sent me home early tonight since *Rumrunner* wasn't busy. December is a weird month for tourism on Smuggler's Hideaway. During the *Mermaid Treasure Hunt,* the weekend before Christmas, it's busy, and at Christmas and New Year's, it's extremely busy. But otherwise? Quiet as you'd expect an island outside the Summer vacation months to be.

The house is nice and quiet. Adele is with Zane's mom since he's playing poker with his brothers at Eli's. Knowing the Raider brothers, there's a good chance I get a call from the police asking me to pick him up.

"It's you and me tonight, Boozer." I pet my dog and switch on the television.

After five minutes of scrolling through channels, I realize it's too quiet in the house. I miss the sound of Adele's laughs. When she smiles, Zane's entire face lights up with happiness. Does he realize how attached he is to his baby girl?

The door bangs open and I startle awake. Boozer barks and rushes to the front door.

"Shush, Boozer boy. Don't wake my baby girl."

Zane tries to pet the dog but he stumbles to the side and slams into the wall.

"Who put that there?"

I giggle. Someone's been drinking.

His head whips up and he grins at me. "Sloane. You're home."

Hope tries to spark, but I squash it. Home? This isn't home. This is Zane's home. Not mine. I want a home, but I won't steal his. Not when my welcome is contingent on being his nanny. When he doesn't need me anymore? I swallow. I don't want to think about it.

"How's Adele?"

"I'm sure she's fine."

His brow wrinkles. "You don't know?"

He tries to kick off his shoes but stumbles again and ends up on his ass. Boozer licks his face but he shoves my dog away. "Ew. Gross."

Boozer thinks this is a game and dances around Zane, trying to kiss him while Zane bats him away. Or tries to. His arms are flailing and, if this is a game, Boozer's winning.

I offer him a hand. "Need help?"

"Why would I?" He glances around. "Huh. I'm on the floor."

"How much did you have to drink?"

"It's not my fault," he grumbles. "My asshole brothers insisted I drink a shot every time I mentioned Adele. Adele's mine, you know."

I pull him to his feet and he crashes into me. I brace my legs to keep from falling backward at his weight. It's a good thing I have years of practice dealing with drunks because otherwise we'd be a pile of limbs on the floor.

"I know Adele's yours."

"No. No. No." He shakes his head. "Adele is my baby. I'm her daddy."

I nod. "I know."

He shakes my shoulders. "You're not listening. Adele is my baby. I'm her biolog…biologi…biological father."

Warmth spreads through me. "You got the results of the paternity test?"

"Yeah." He smiles and the two dimples on his left cheek make an appearance. The love he has for his daughter makes him gorgeous. Even drunk, with his face flushed and his hair matted to his head.

"Let's go see my baby girl."

He starts for the nursery but I stop him.

"Adele isn't here."

"Isn't here?" he shouts. "Was she kidnapped? Did my asshole brothers steal her?"

"She's at your mom's, remember?"

"I have an idea," he announces.

Please don't say have sex, because there's no way I can resist him at this moment. Not when his face is lit up with happiness that Adele is his biological daughter. A man who's happy about a baby being his? It's catnip to me.

"Let's go get her."

"You want to go to your mother's to get your daughter?"

"My daughter." He sighs. "Yeah."

"You're drunk."

"I've only had a wee bit to drink."

I laugh at his imitation of a Scottish accent. "A wee bit?"

"It's what they say in Edinburgh when they've been drinking all night."

"You've been to Edinburgh?"

Zane's traveled a lot. He's always jetting off somewhere for a new adventure. Canoeing on the Rio Grande, ziplining in Costa Rica, chasing gorillas in Uganda. Zane has seen and done it all.

I'm not jealous of the traveling. Growing up with a mother who couldn't live longer than a year in one place cured me of any desire to travel. But the locations he visited? How I long to visit Edinburgh, London, Dublin, Amsterdam – if only I didn't have to travel to get to those cities.

"A few times." He shrugs and I nearly drop him since he can't make any movement without stumbling.

"I want to hear all about it."

"I'll tell you and Adele all about it." He scans the room. "Where is Adele?"

The forgetful drunk has entered the room. "She's at your mom's."

"Let's go get her."

"You're drunk."

"So? I'm a smuggler."

"Being a smuggler doesn't mean you can drink and drive."

Smuggler's Hideaway is pretty lax on rules. Public nudity? Slap on the wrist. Playing loud music in the middle of the night? A stern talking to and a reminder to invite your neighbors next time. Not picking up after your dog? A day of community service cleaning the beach.

But drinking and driving is a whole different kettle of fish. It's dangerous, and Smugglers don't abide danger – especially when Sammy the seal enjoys sunbathing in the middle of the street.

"You can drive. You haven't been drinking."

"I haven't?" I'm not lying. I'm merely leading him in the wrong direction.

"Damn." His shoulders fall. "I miss my baby girl."

He seriously needs to stop with the sweet dad routine or I'll fall in love with him. And falling in love with Zane Raider will only lead to heartbreak.

Considering Zane and his brothers visit the bar regularly, I'd have to quit my job. And maybe leave the island. The only place I've ever felt at home.

Nope. It's better to keep my hands to myself.

Zane slumps against me before letting out a snore. Great. He fell asleep in my arms.

"Come on, daddy. Let's get you to bed."

"I'm not tired," he mumbles.

"We can watch television in bed."

Since I can hear Zane's television blaring sports in his room at all hours of the night and day, I figure this will get him moving. And I'm right. He shuffles toward the hallway.

I secure his arm around my shoulder and wrap my arm around his waist as I help him walk. Or, rather, I help him not slam into walls and doors.

By the time we reach his bedroom, I'm cursing how heavy he is. His broad shoulders may be pretty to look at, but they're freaking heavy to keep steady.

"Here's your bed." I gently push him and he collapses.

My job here is done. "Good night."

"Wait." He shackles my wrist. "Watch television with me."

I glance around the room. There's a bed and a dresser in here. No chair for me to sit on. There's only one place for me, but laying on the bed with Zane is a bad idea with disaster written all over it.

"I think I'll go to bed."

He slaps the bed next to him. "Guess what? I have a bed right here."

"In my own bed. To sleep."

"Come on." He tugs on my wrist. "Just for a little while."

"It's not a good idea."

"It's an excellent idea," he declares and pulls on my wrist until I land on the bed next to him.

Welp. I guess I'm watching television with Zane in his bed. That smells of him. I inhale his oaky musk scent and a little burst of excitement travels through me. I'd roll around in his scent if I could.

"What do you want to watch?"

His response? A snore.

I bite my tongue before I laugh and wake him up. I pry his hand away from my wrist before sliding toward the edge of the bed. I'm nearly there when Zane rolls over and throws an arm around me.

"Zane." I try pushing his arm off me but he merely tightens his hold.

I keep trying but eventually give up. Guess I'm sleeping with Zane tonight.

I make myself as comfortable as possible, considering I have a fifty-pound arm draped over me. I'll probably lay here half the night until Zane rolls over and frees me. But I close my eyes and fall asleep.

Chapter 19

"Apparently, my pillow turned into Sloane last night. Not complaining."

ZANE

I snuggle into my pillow. Hold on. This isn't a pillow. My pillows don't smell of strawberries and sunshine.

I inhale a deep breath. Strawberries and sunshine. It's Sloane's scent.

Sloane? Has she been in my bed?

I sift through last night's memories. Poker with my brothers. Shots with my brothers. Oh, so many shots. Coming home. Stumbling drunk to my bed.

And not letting Sloane leave.

My resistance to my beautiful nanny crashed to the floor last night. I wanted her in my bed and I made it happen.

I tighten my arm around her and bury my face in her neck. Too bad she's dressed, but I'll take Sloane anyway I can get her.

"Zane."

"I'm right here."

"Zane," she murmurs again as she rubs her legs together.

"Sloane?"

She moans in her sleep.

Holy shit. Is Sloane having a sex dream about me?

I want to roll her over, strip her clothes off, and sink deep inside of her. I reach to roll her over but drop my arm when I remember she's sleeping. I'm not taking advantage of her.

But then she wiggles her ass against my cock. It springs into action. Hard and heavy and ready to get this show on the road.

"Sloane." I shake her shoulder. "Wake up, Sloane. You're dreaming."

Her eyes flutter open. "I'm dreaming?"

"Yes."

She scans the room. "Why am I in your bed?" She groans. "Now, I remember. Someone had too much to drink and didn't want to sleep alone."

I shrug. I have no defense.

"Why did you wake me?"

"You were dreaming."

"Dreaming? What was I dreaming about?" Her eyes go out of focus as she tries to remember.

I can do this. I can answer without embarrassing her. It won't be my first tightrope act.

"I'm not sure."

She lifts an eyebrow. "You don't know what I was dreaming about, but you woke me? Was I having a nightmare?"

"No. And you should never wake someone in the middle of a nightmare."

"Why did you wake me, Zane? You're holding back. What is it?"

Damn. Guess I'm not as good at balancing on a tightrope as I thought.

"You were wiggling and moving around."

"Why would you wake me…." Her voice trails off, and she drops her chin to her chest. "Tell me I wasn't having a sex dream."

"You weren't having a sex dream."

"Tell me I wasn't having a sex dream about you."

"You weren't…" She lifts her gaze to mine and I trail off with a shrug.

"Could this be any more embarrassing?"

"I'd find it pretty embarrassing if you were having a sex dream about another man while in my bed."

She snorts. "As if any other man can capture my attention."

Say what? I roll over until I'm on top of her. "Have I captured your attention?"

She rolls her eyes. "You know you have."

I don't know shit. Until she moved in to help me with Adele, she ignored me or snapped at me. I thought she hated me. But then I learned about her asshole dad.

I brush the hair from her forehead. "I'm not your dad. I'm not some player who would abandon a child."

"I know."

My heart squeezes at her admission. "Does this mean you'll let me make you feel good?"

She squirms beneath me. "It's not a good idea."

I press my hard cock into her stomach. "I think it's an excellent idea."

"My friends are friends with your friends. I work for your sister-in-law. I'm your temporary nanny. We live together. How many more reasons do you need to realize this is a bad idea?"

I've never had to convince a woman to have sex with me before. I'm not certain how to proceed. But I won't push her. This has to be her decision. I won't be a regret.

"I don't do relationships."

She drops her gaze to my chest. "I know."

I pinch her chin and force her to meet my gaze. "But I don't run away either. I won't fuck you in this bed and then ignore you."

"You can't ignore me. I'm your daughter's nanny."

Which is why I should let this go and walk away. If we have sex and she gets upset or runs away, I'm screwed. I need her. Her help, I amend. I need her help. Not her.

"Okay," I give in. "But at least let me give you an orgasm."

Her eyes flare and her breath hitches. "An orgasm?"

"I won't fuck you. I'll keep my cock in my clothes. But I can't stand the way you're writhing against me. You need relief and I can give it to you."

"You're going to give me an orgasm but keep your dick to yourself?"

It's cute how she says dick. I bet I could get her to say the word cock during sex.

"I can use my fingers or my mouth." I waggle my eyebrows. "What'll it be?"

"This isn't a good idea," she says but she's rubbing herself against me. I can feel the heat of her core through my jeans.

"You can walk away now."

She studies me for a moment. "What if I want a non-self-induced orgasm?"

"I'm your man." Those words feel right. I force the thought away. I'm not Sloane's man. I don't do relationships. Except I have a baby daughter now. I guess I do some relationships.

"Okay," she gasps out and I start to shimmy down her body.

She tugs on my ears to stop me. "But this is our secret. You tell no one and I'll tell no one."

My stomach sours. I'm no one's secret. But I find myself nodding. I want to taste Sloane more than anything. Besides, what we do in this bed is no one's business.

"Deal," I murmur before sliding down her body. "I want to taste you." Her eyes flare.

I draw her sweats with her panties down her legs. Her shapely, smooth legs I want to feel wrapped around me. My cock pulses in my jeans in agreement.

"Spread your legs, sweetness."

She bites her bottom lip and stares at me for a long moment. Is she shy in bed? She won't be shy once she realizes how good I can make her feel.

I tap her ankle and she opens for me. "Wider, sweetness. My shoulders need to fit."

I draw my hands up her legs until I nearly reach her core before retreating. I repeat the action a few times until her breaths are shallow.

I drop my chin to hide my grin. I don't want her thinking I'm laughing at her.

I fit my shoulders between her legs and use my fingers to open her up wide to me. I drag my nose along her slit and inhale. Strawberries and sunshine.

I wonder if she tastes as good as she smells. Time to find out.

I circle her clit with my tongue and she jumps. I chuckle as I place a hand over her hips to keep her right where I want her.

I tease her clit with my tongue until she threads her hands through my hair and yanks. Only then do I latch on and suck. She moans long and hard.

I continue to suck and nibble on her hard nub until her legs are trembling.

"Zane," she wheezes.

"Right here, sweetness."

I don't demand she tell me what she wants. There will be time for demands in the future. I frown. Future? This is a one off.

All my sexual encounters are one and done. But I don't want to lump Sloane into the same pile as all the other women I've been with. She's different.

Shit. Am I falling for her?

I force those thoughts away. I promised Sloane an orgasm, and I always keep my promises.

I move on to her core and stab my tongue into her pussy. I was right. She tastes delicious. Sweeter than any pastry from *Pirate's Pastries.* I could get addicted to her taste.

"Zane. Zane. Zane," she chants.

I lift my head to meet her gaze. "Right here, sweetness."

She lifts her ass and uses the hold on my hair to shove my face into her pussy. I chuckle as I return my attention to her hot, wet core. I pump my tongue in and out of her and her walls tremble around me.

She's close, and I promised her an orgasm. I press my thumb to her clit and make circles while I continue to eat her pussy.

Her fingers tighten on my hair. "I'm…" She doesn't finish the sentence before she detonates in my mouth. "Zane," she moans.

I draw out her climax with my tongue until she collapses on the bed.

I get to my knees and she stares up at me with a smile on her face. It's a smile I want to see in my bed every day.

Every day? Damn. I am falling for Sloane.

Chapter 20

"I can add 'dodging Raider family walk-ins' to my new skill set."

SLOANE

"Hello!"

My eyes fly open at the shouted greeting.

Zane groans. "It's my mom."

"Your mom?" I screech. "We're in bed together, and your mom is here?"

Hurt flashes in his eyes before he blinks and it's gone. Why would he be hurt? Does he want his mom to catch us? I will never understand Zane Raider.

"Relax. She won't invade my bedroom."

Woof!

Uh oh. Boozer's awake. And I'm not in my room to contain him. I need to get out of here.

I try to roll out of bed but my legs get tangled in the sheets. I kick at the material. It gives way and – boom! – I crash to the floor.

"Are you okay, Zane? Do you need help?"

"I do not need help getting out of bed, Mom."

"I heard a thump."

"I stubbed my toe on the corner of the bed."

I push the covers off of me and squeak when I realize I'm naked from the waist down.

"Do you want my mom to hear you?" Zane asks between bouts of laughter.

I glare at him. "I should have gotten dressed last night."

I should not have let Zane go down on me is what I should have done. But I couldn't resist. I woke up wet and wanting from a dream about him and then – poof! – he was there offering to give me an orgasm.

I couldn't resist. And who could blame me? Zane has been voted sexiest man on the island – trust me, it's a thing – and he was above me, all hard and growly. Of course, I gave in. I'm only human.

He shrugs. "It's not my fault you passed out after one orgasm."

My brow wrinkles. "One orgasm? You make one orgasm sound bad."

"I wanted to give you another one with my fingers but you fell asleep."

I blink my eyes as I try to compute what he's saying. He wanted to give me another orgasm? In my experience, men only give orgasms in order to get their own orgasm.

But Zane didn't ask for anything in return. He kept his cock in his pants the way he promised. Maybe he is a gentleman and not a player after all.

"Are you decent?" Zane's mom asks from directly outside his door.

I bury my face in my hands. How did I go from having the best orgasm in my life to humiliation? How?

"Not yet."

"You always did enjoy sleeping naked. Even as a little boy, you hated wearing clothes to bed. In fact, you hated wearing clothes at all. We had to make a rule for you to wait until you were home to strip. Whenever my friends would drop by, you'd be sprinting around the house with your dick hanging in the breeze."

"Mom," Zane groans. "Please don't talk about my dick."

"Why? I'm your mother. I gave birth to you. I cleaned your diapers. I am acquainted with your anatomy."

I shove my fist in my mouth before I burst out laughing. No wonder the Raider brothers are crazy. They come by it naturally. From their mother.

"Don't you dare laugh," Zane growls at me.

"I hope your daughter won't take after you," I whisper. "Racing around naked all the time."

"About Adele." Zane raises his voice for his mom. "I have news."

"I'll let you get dressed and then you can tell me your news."

He sighs. "She already knows. My brothers told her. The assholes."

I wish I had brothers I could call assholes. But no. It's just me and my mother. Correction. It's just me.

He rolls out of bed without incident. Since he passed out in his clothes last night, he's already dressed.

"Take your time."

As soon as the door closes behind him, I jump to my feet and search the room for my sweats and panties. I can't find the panties, so I pull on my sweats without underwear.

Once I'm dressed, I creep to the door. I ensure it's silent in the hallway before I inch the door open and peek outside. Awesome. It's empty.

I rush to the bathroom. I glance in the mirror and slap my hand over my mouth before I can scream. My hair is pointing up in all directions, and my makeup is smeared all over my face. I don't want to think about how bad my breath must smell.

I guess there's a bright side to falling out of bed. Zane didn't have a chance to smell my morning breath.

Maybe I should hide in the bathroom until Zane's mom leaves. It wouldn't be odd since I usually work late.

There's a knock on the door. "Do you want chocolate chip or blueberry pancakes?" Zane's mom asks.

My stomach rumbles. I guess there'll be no hiding in the bathroom for me today.

"Blueberry."

"Good. Zane always wants chocolate chip. Maybe with your influence, he'll eat healthier."

My influence? What does she think I'm doing in his house? I'm the nanny. Except she arrived while I was pretty much naked in my boss's bed.

"Hurry up, dear. Zane may prefer chocolate chip, but he'll eat your blueberry pancakes if he has the chance."

"Be right there!"

I wait until I hear her footsteps retreat down the hall before making my way out of the bathroom. I expect Boozer to rush me but he's nowhere to be found.

"If you're searching for Boozer, he's outside," Zane says when I enter the kitchen.

He hands me a cup of coffee and his mom cheers.

"Why is she cheering?" I whisper.

"Because I'm happy. Adele is Zane's baby girl."

I have a feeling she's lying, but I am not digging deeper into the topic. I'm afraid to know why she's happy and cheering.

"Good morning, Mrs. Raider."

"Call me Jessica. You don't refer to members of the family by their last name."

"I'm not a member of the family."

No matter how much I may wish it to be otherwise. I'm a family of one.

Jessica waves my comment away. "Of course, you're part of this family. You're Zane's…nanny."

"Mom," Zane growls.

She bats her eyelashes at him. "What, dear?"

"Stop causing trouble."

She clutches her chest. "Me? Cause trouble? I have six boys who cause trouble."

"Where do you think we learned it from?"

She giggles and returns her attention to the stove, where she's making pancakes. I inhale the sugary scent into my lungs and moan. "Those smell delicious."

"Are you hungry?" she asks. "Did you have an arduous night?"

"Enough, Mom," Zane orders. "Sloane is my nanny. She's not my girlfriend."

Those words pierce through my heart and threaten to break me in two, but I hold strong. He's not wrong. We are not a couple. He certainly didn't make any promises last night before he whipped off my pants and made me climax in his mouth.

"Nevertheless, she should come to Christmas at our house."

"I don't want to intrude."

Zane squeezes my hand. "She's right. You should come to Christmas at our house."

"No." I shake my head. "Christmas is for families."

"And since you don't have any family, you'll be celebrating with us."

I close my eyes to stop the pain from hitting me at his words. They're true, but I don't need a reminder.

"I'm working on Christmas." I nearly forgot all about my job at *Rumrunner* at the invitation. No one's invited me over for Christmas since I was a teenager and Mom flew off to Miami to spend the weekend with her boyfriend.

"*Rumrunner* doesn't open until the evening on Christmas. You can spend the morning and lunch with us before you go to work."

Jessica sets a platter of pancakes on the table. "Excellent. It's all figured out."

I didn't agree to anything, but when I open my mouth to say as much, she slays me with a look that makes me feel guilty down to my toes. I don't dare speak.

She pats my arm. "Now sit down and eat. We can discuss our costumes for the Smuggler's Holiday Masquerade Dance. I'm thinking we go as mermaids and mermen this year."

"I'm actually bartending at the dance. I volunteered since *Rumrunner* is closed on Christmas Eve."

And I had nowhere else to go. I'm not about to attend a dance with a room full of couples in love by myself. It'd be different if the dance happened in the summer with droves of tourists. While there are tourists who attend the Masquerade Dance, they're mostly couples who have decided to escape their families and spend the holiday on the island.

"You'll have to miss the dance this year, but next year I expect you there."

"I—"

"WAH!" Adele cries through the baby monitor and cuts me off.

Zane starts to stand but Jessica waves him off. "Let me spend a few more minutes with my granddaughter." She sweeps out of the room and I can finally breathe again.

"What is happening?"

Zane piles a bunch of chocolate chip pancakes on his plate. "No idea."

"Zane."

He shoves a forkful of pancake into his mouth and shrugs.

I frown at him. He's lying. I know he is. But about what? And why?

Why would Zane want me to attend Christmas with his family? He flees from the word relationship.

Maybe he's keen to ensure I remain his nanny?

I don't know. All I do know is he's confusing the smuggler out of me.

Chapter 21

"Nothing says holiday spirit like realizing you're screwed (in the good way)."

ZANE

"There you go, baby girl," I murmur to Adele as I finish dressing her. "All set for your first Christmas."

"How was the ball last night?" Sloane asks as she stumbles into the room.

She's dressed for the holiday in a black skirt and red blouse. She's beautiful and all I can think about is tearing those clothes off her. My cock twitches in agreement.

Unfortunately, Sloane's avoided meeting my gaze since the other night. She needs time to realize our relationship has changed.

I grit my teeth and force my cock under control before lifting Adele from the changing table and placing her on my hip. "We didn't go."

I couldn't stand the thought of Adele being with a babysitter on Christmas Eve. And there was no way I was taking my baby girl to a ball on Smuggler's Hideaway, where the moonshine flows and the pranks abound.

"You didn't go. Why…." She trails off with a gasp. "Oh my mermaid. Adele is adorable in her Christmas dress."

Pride for my daughter fills me. "She is, isn't she?"

She holds up a finger. "Hold on."

I make my way to the living room with Adele as Sloane rushes to her bedroom. She hurries back carrying a wrapped present.

"Adele is too young to enjoy opening presents, but I couldn't let her first Christmas pass without one."

"Here." I hand her my baby girl. "Help her open it."

She hesitates for a moment before sitting on the floor with Adele between her legs. I dig my phone out of my pocket and snap a few pictures as she helps my baby girl open her present.

"It's a blanket with a mermaid on it," she explains to Adele, who shoves the material into her mouth. Sloane barks out a laugh and I snap another picture.

The picture of Sloane laughing with Adele sitting between her legs nearly takes my breath away. This is what I want. This is what I've been searching for. No cliff dive or base jump could ever bring me the satisfaction I feel while watching the woman I'm falling for interact with my daughter.

Sloane squeezes my knee. "Are you okay? You're pale. You didn't catch the flu going around, did you? I don't want Adele getting sick."

I inhale deep breaths until my heart rate slows down to normal. "I'm okay."

I'm shocked as shit by the epiphany I just had, but I'm okay. I'll be even better after I convince Sloane to give me a chance.

"Time for you to open your present." I motion to the small tree on the table.

Between having a dog that thinks everything not nailed down is a toy to play with and a baby I'm convinced is going to start crawling any minute, we decided not to put a tree up this year. Which was fine with me. I normally don't decorate for the holidays.

But as I scan the living room devoid of Christmas decorations, I realize I made a mistake. I should have let Sloane decorate the way she wanted to. Decorations make a house into a home. Next year.

"You didn't have to get me a present," Sloane says but she jumps to her feet and hurries to the tree to grab the present.

I snap another picture as she tears into the wrapping paper. She gasps when the present is revealed. "This is too much."

"It's more reliable than the cheap, plastic thing you're wearing now."

She glances at her watch. "I was saving to buy a better one."

"Now, you don't need to." I dig the watch out of the box. "Let me put it on you."

She holds out her arm. I secure the watch around her wrist. While she studies it, I rub circles with my thumb around her pulse point. She shivers in response.

"This is too much."

"It wasn't expensive." Because I didn't buy her the Tag Heuer I wanted to. I knew she'd lose her mind at such an expensive gift.

"But it's pretty."

I tuck a strand of hair behind her ear. "A pretty watch for a pretty woman."

She gazes up at me from beneath her lashes. When she licks her lip, I groan and lean toward her. But before my lips can meet hers, she jumps to her feet.

"Your present!"

"I don't need a present."

She ignores me as she hurries to her bedroom. She returns carrying a wrapped box. "It's not much but…"

My heart warms. We hadn't discussed giving each other presents. I assumed she wouldn't buy me one since she hasn't had a family to buy presents for in a long time.

I snatch the box from her. "I'm sure I'll love it."

I place Adele between my legs and show her how to tear the wrapping paper off but she's not interested. I can't wait for the Christmases and birthdays when she's excited for presents. I'm going to spoil her rotten.

Sloane plops down next to me and lifts Adele into her lap. I open the present and my jaw drops open.

"You don't like it?" Sloane bites her bottom lip. "I thought—"

"I love it!" I lift the sweatshirt out of the box and stand up to put it on. "What do you think? How do I look?"

She beams at me. "Like the world's best daddy." Which is what the sweatshirt says.

"I'm wearing it to the Raider family Christmas." I check the time. "Speaking of which, we need to go. I don't want to be late for Mom's Christmas brunch."

She jumps into action. "Did you pack Adele's baby bag? Never mind. I'll do it."

She returns with a packed bag in less than a minute. My brow wrinkles. "Why is the diaper bag bigger than normal?"

"I added an extra outfit in case this one doesn't last. We don't want Miss Adele to not look perfect on her first Christmas."

Warmth spreads throughout me. Sloane loves my baby girl. This is proof, Sloane is worth taking a chance on. Even for someone like me, who usually doesn't do relationships.

We arrive at my mother's house fifteen minutes later. Sloane's eyes widen when she notices the amount of cars in the driveway.

"Did your mom invite the entire island of Smuggler's Hideaway to brunch?"

I chuckle. "Nope. It's the family."

She shakes her head. "Remind me to never have six children."

"How many children do you want?"

She shrugs. "Two or three. But I have to find a man first."

Sweetness, you have found your man. You just don't know it yet.

While she rescues Adele from the car seat, I grab the diaper bag and the bag of presents.

"Oh no." Sloane's eyes widen when she notices the presents. "I didn't buy any presents. I was going to steal a bottle of whiskey from the bar but I forgot. Maybe I should go back to your house."

I grasp her hand. "Don't be silly. These presents are from us."

I hold her hand as we enter Mom's house. The second we're inside, cheers erupt.

"I knew it! Pay up, suckers." Miles holds out his hand.

Jaxon rolls his eyes. "I didn't bet."

"And I agreed with you," Rhett adds as Eli nods in agreement.

"Kai Raider," Sloane growls. "Hold the mistletoe over my head and see what happens. I dare you."

Kai gasps. "How do you see me?"

She points to the mirror over the fireplace. "I've been watching men try to sneak up on me since I was fourteen."

I frown. "Fourteen?"

"You've met my mom. You can't be surprised."

I growl. "Did your mom's boyfriends touch you?"

Stuart sweeps in and steals Adele from Sloane's arms. "Just getting my granddaughter out of harm's way before blood is shed."

Stuart steps back but Sloane scowls at him. "Who are you?"

"Sloane, this is my step-dad, Stuart."

Her face pales. "Sorry, I didn't realize. I mean, I know Jessica is remarried, but I didn't recognize you. Which is crazy since I have seen you before. On multiple occasions in the bar and around the island. Oh, mermaid, someone stop me."

I chuckle and throw an arm around her shoulders. "You're adorable."

"Ugh." Miles moans. "Another one bites the dust. Can we have one occasion in this family where a brother isn't mooning over some woman?"

Jaxon fiddles with his glasses. "I believe you're mooning over a woman at this very moment."

"Burn." Kai licks his finger and makes a sizzling sound.

Sloane barks out a laugh. "Are we discussing Hazel?" At my nod, she shakes her head. "You are going to have to do a bunch of groveling to get her back." She rubs her hands together. "Shall we bet on how long it'll take?"

"I don't like you," Miles mumbles as he flees the room.

I growl and set off after him but Sloane captures my wrist to stop me. "You love me and you know it!" she shouts after him. "I'm your favorite bartender."

Screw falling for this woman. Consider me fallen. I love Sloane Wilder. No other woman could put up with my brothers' shit with a grin on her face. And shovel their shit right back at them. Not to mention how protective she is of my daughter.

"Miles Raider, I'm throwing away your Christmas present."

At Mom's shout, I rush to the kitchen with Sloane and my brothers. Mom slams a bottle of chocolate syrup onto the counter. On top of the bottle sits an elf with his pants pulled down as if he's using the bottle as a toilet.

Sloane buries her face in my shoulder, her body shaking as she tries to contain her laughter. My brothers and I don't bother trying to contain our laughter.

Mom glares at us. "This isn't funny."

Miles smirks. "It's a little funny."

She grabs a rolling pin and rushes after him. He scurries away while singing, "I'm the gingerbread man. You can't catch me."

Sloane smiles up at me. "You were right. Christmas at your mom's house is not to be missed."

I'm glad she thinks so because if I have my way, she'll be spending all of her future Christmases here with me and Adele.

And I intend to have my way.

Chapter 22

"I asked for a quiet day. The universe laughed."

SLOANE

Zane hesitates at the door. "Are you sure you don't mind babysitting Adele today?"

Did he forget I'm the nanny? "I babysit her every day while you work."

"But it's your day off."

Rumrunner is officially closed today. It's a rare occurrence, but Harper wanted to give us time to recover from Christmas. The bar was packed on Christmas and Boxing Day.

It was crazier than normal, which is saying a lot for Smuggler's Hideaway. I don't want to see another naked mermaid or find another piece of glitter in my clothes for at least two weeks. Too bad New Year's Eve is coming up.

"It's fine. My only plans for today are to relax with Boozer and Adele."

"If you change your mind, call Mom. She'll jump at the chance to spend some time with Adele."

She'd also use the opportunity to try and push me and Zane together. I cottoned on to her play at Christmas. She wants Zane to settle down, and apparently, Little Miss Matchmaker has chosen me as Zane's partner. Doesn't she realize her son will never settle down?

Although, he did cancel all of his holiday plans for Adele. He was planning a trip to Iceland. There's an active volcano he wants to hike. I shiver. An active volcano? Is he nuts? But he stayed home instead. He's even going into the distillery to attend a meeting he'd normally skip.

"Go," I tell Zane. "If you're late for another meeting, Eli and Rhett will have your head."

"Nah. I'll tell them Adele had a blowout."

I snuggle the baby closer. "Don't you dare use this precious girl as an excuse."

He sighs. "Fine. I'm going. As soon as you promise to call Mom if you need her."

I roll my eyes. "I'll call your mom if I need her."

He waves before leaving.

"Finally, he's gone. What do you want to do? Watch a scary movie? Go for a pub crawl?"

Adele's response is a big yawn. "I hear you, sweetie pie. I'm tired, too. Should we take a nap?"

I push to my feet. As much as I'd enjoy sleeping all cuddled up to Adele on the sofa, it's too dangerous. I'm not allowing this precious girl to get trapped between the sofa cushions or suffocate on my watch.

I lay Adele in her crib before shuffling down the hall to my bedroom. Boozer jumps on the bed and I cuddle into his side as I fall asleep.

Ding dong. Ding dong.

The doorbell rings and I groan. Who could it possibly be? Zane's mom – any member of his family, really – would barge inside without knocking. And, as we've established, I have no family. Flying pirates, I hope it's not Mom.

I roll out of bed and make my way to the nursery. Adele is awake and waiting for me in her crib. I settle her on my hip and go answer the door.

"Who are you?" I ask the stranger on the porch.

The woman scowls at me. "I'm the mother."

My eyes widen as I inch backwards. "You're Adele's mother?"

"Yes. And I want her back."

"You want her back?"

"Yep. I'm on break from college and have time for her now."

"You have time for her now?"

"Are you going to stare at me with your mouth gaping open and repeat everything I say?"

I slam my mouth shut.

"Are you going to give me my baby or what?"

Or what. Definitely or what.

No way, no how is this woman taking Adele. It would break Zane's heart. And I wouldn't walk away unscathed either. This little girl has wormed her way into my heart.

I'm not letting this woman treat Adele the way my mother treated me – as an inconvenience she only had time for when she was bored.

"You can't show up here and make demands. Adele isn't a toy. You can't play with her when you want and then dump her when you're bored."

She stomps her foot. "Adele is mine. Give her to me."

She wants the baby, and yet she hasn't looked at Adele once. She hasn't asked how she's doing. She hasn't shown concern for her whatsoever.

She's also acting like a child. Stomping her foot and making demands.

"How old are you?"

She flips her hair over her shoulder. "What difference does it make?"

She's right. It doesn't make any difference.

I inhale a deep breath and blow it – along with all my anger at the situation – out. Being angry and fighting with this woman is not going to help.

"Let's start over. Hi, I'm Sloane. And your name is?"

"Are you Zane's latest piece?" She rolls her eyes. "He's such a player."

I nearly nod to agree with her, but I'm actually not sure she's correct. Not any longer, at least. Zane hasn't had any interest in any women since I moved in with him, and it's been a month.

Except you.

I push those thoughts away. I'm not going to reminisce over what Zane and I did while standing in front of his baby mama.

"I'm the nanny."

"Nanny? And Zane hasn't tried to sleep with you yet?"

I scowl at her.

She leans closer to study my face. "Although, you might be a bit old for him."

"Old? I'm thirty-one."

"Exactly." She nods. "Old."

She's such a pleasant woman. What did Zane see in her? I scan her body. She has big boobs and a small waist. I think I answered my own question.

She glances at her watch. "I don't have all day. My plane departs in a few hours."

"I don't care when your plane departs. You are not taking Adele."

"She's my baby. Do you understand?"

"I understand you gave birth to her. I also understand you abandoned her."

"I didn't abandon her."

"You gave her to Zane and rushed off before he could ask you any questions."

She rolls her eyes. "I'm not a monster."

"Abandoning your child with a man who didn't know about her existence isn't going to win you Mother of the Year."

"I don't know what the big deal is. The baby is obviously doing fine."

"Adele," I grit out. "Adele is doing well."

"Are you going to give me my baby or are we going to stand outside on the porch and argue all morning?"

I scan our surroundings. Several of the neighbors are standing on their porches, eavesdropping on the drama playing out. I don't want to be the cause of everyone on Smuggler's Hideaway gossiping about Zane.

I step back and motion her inside.

She follows me into the living room and studies the area. "This place hasn't changed a bit."

My stomach sours at the reminder of how she's been here before. I don't need the reminder. I'm literally holding proof they had sex in my arms.

Jealousy slams into me. I try to shake it off. I don't have any claim to Zane.

You've kissed and had sex.

Those things don't mean anything to Zane. I think. We never discussed what happened that night in his bed.

Boozer comes flying out of my room barking. He skids to a halt when he notices the woman – who still hasn't given me her name! With a growl, he positions himself in front of me and sits on my feet.

"What is this thing?"

I scratch behind his ears. "This is my dog, Boozer."

"Dog? He doesn't resemble any dog I've ever seen before."

Boozer growls at her and she inches backward.

"Is he rabid? Maybe he should be put down."

I glare at her. "My dog doesn't need to be put down."

"Are you certain? He's drooling all over your shoes." She laughs at her own joke and claps her hands.

Uh oh. She did it now. Clapping hands is a signal for Boozer to come. He bounds toward her. He jumps on her and lands with his front paws on her shoulders. She shrieks.

"Get him off of me! Get him off!"

Boozer thinks she's playing with him and licks her face. She tries to shove him away, but when my dog doesn't budge, she ends up falling back on her ass.

The door behind her opens and Zane marches inside. "What the hell is going on here?" He frowns at the woman on the floor. "What are you doing here, Daisy?"

Daisy! That's her name.

"Daisy wants Adele back but I refused," I explain. I narrow my eyes at her. "Adele isn't a toy you can abandon when you're tired of her."

She rolls her eyes. "Not the toy metaphor again."

She holds out her hand to Zane to help her up but he ignores her to stand next to me and crosses his arms over his chest.

Relief knocks into me with such force, my knees wobble. Zane isn't helping Daisy. He's standing with me.

Chapter 23

"Never underestimate my brothers during an intel op."

ZANE

I stand next to Sloane, who is glaring at Daisy as if she's ready to beat her down. She's not letting anyone take Adele from her.

I love how possessive she is of Adele. I love how she cherishes my daughter as if she were her own. I love Sloane. Plain and simple. And I'm not letting anyone ruin our family. Especially not a woman who abandoned this innocent little baby.

I wait until Daisy stands before addressing her. "Why are you here?"

She points at Boozer. "Her dog attacked me!"

Sloane rolls her eyes. "He didn't attack you. He thought you needed some loving." She snaps her fingers and her dog immediately rushes to her side. "Bedroom." Boozer whines. "Now." He hangs his head as he trots off to the bedroom. He's a good dog.

I repeat my question. "Why are you here?"

Daisy clears her throat. "I want Adele back."

My heart races. She wants to steal my baby. I can't live without Adele. She's my pride and joy.

Ice fills my veins. No one is taking Adele from me. Not even her so-called mother.

"Why?"

"Why?" Daisy's nose wrinkles. "Because she's my baby."

"A baby you haven't once asked to hold since this whole charade began," Sloane mutters.

"She was your baby when you left her with me," I remind Daisy.

She sighs. "I had finals. I didn't have time for a baby then. But now I do."

I fist my hands before I wrap them around her neck and choke her. She didn't have time for Adele, so she abandoned her? Adele is her daughter. She should have made time for her baby.

"Adele isn't…"

Daisy holds up her hand to stop Sloane. "I don't understand why you're speaking. You don't have anything to do with this situation."

Pain flashes in Sloane's eyes before it's replaced with anger. She grits her teeth. "I'm the woman who's been caring for your child while you've been goofing off."

"Goofing off? Are you deaf, old lady? I was studying for finals." She sniffs at Sloane. "You probably wouldn't know what those are. You don't strike me as the type of person to attend college."

"Here." Sloane hands me Adele. "I can't beat Daisy to a pulp with a baby in my arms."

She marches toward Daisy but I shackle her wrist to stop her. "I thought you were anti-violence."

She rears back. "What made you think such a thing? Was it the way I wield a baseball bat at guys hitting on me at the bar? Or how I got in trouble in high school for shoving Patsy into a locker?"

"Anti-violence in front of the baby."

Her shoulders drop. "Oh, yeah." She shuffles back to me and I bite my tongue before I laugh at her. This situation is not a laughing matter.

"You are fucking," Daisy announces.

I growl. "What Sloane and I do inside our house is none of your fucking business."

"Language," Sloane mutters.

"I promise I'll start a swear jar tomorrow, but I can't deal with this bitch without using some strong language."

"Bitch!" Daisy squeals. "You can't call the mother of your child a bitch."

I snort. "I can when the 'mother' abandons her child."

"Would everyone stop saying I abandoned my daughter?" she yells.

"Waaah!" Adele screams.

Sloane takes her from me. "I don't blame you for crying. All this yelling. Why don't we go into your nursery and play?"

She glances up at me and I nod at her. "Go ahead." I kiss Adele's head before Sloane wanders off with her.

Daisy beams at me. "Finally."

"Finally, what?"

"She's gone."

"Who?" I grumble. She better not be referring to Adele.

She flicks her hand. "The floozy."

"The floozy?" I blink. "You're referring to Sloane as the floozy?"

Daisy is the one who fucked me without knowing anything about me, but Sloane – who I had to beg before she'd let me touch her – is the floozy.

"She's obviously trying to catch you."

"Catch me?"

She motions to the house. "You have money. She's a nanny. Everyone knows women only become nannies to snag a rich husband."

Wow. Daisy is full of judgment about everyone except herself.

"I don't want to discuss Sloane. I want to discuss why you're here."

"How many times do I have to say it?" She pouts. "I want the baby back."

She's not getting Adele. As soon as the judge gives me sole custody— Hold on. My lawyer, Siena, hasn't filed for custody yet because we don't have any information about Daisy except her name.

I motion to the sofa. "Why don't we sit down?"

She checks the time. "I really do need to be going."

"Please. We should discuss things."

"What things?" she asks as she sits down.

"Where do you live? Do you want Adele full-time? Or are you bringing her back when school begins again?"

Her mouth gapes open in surprise. I don't blame her. I went from antagonistic to accommodating in the blink of an eye. Smugglers would know I'm up to no good. But she doesn't know me well enough to question my motives.

Guilt has my chest tightening. I share a child with this woman, and yet I don't even know her last name. What kind of dad am I?

The kind of dad who's going to figure it out – there's a knock on the door before my brothers invade – with the help of my family.

Eli screeches to a halt in the living room. He feigns surprise as he looks at Daisy. "Sorry, bro. I didn't realize you had company."

"This is Daisy. She's Adele's mom."

Eli saunters forward while smoothing a hand down his tie. I've never been more glad my oldest brother knows how to play the part of the rich billionaire he is.

"I'm sorry," he says as he offers her his hand. "I didn't catch your last name."

"Simmons," she mutters as she stares up at him with her mouth hanging open.

He shakes her hand before sitting on the coffee table in front of her. "And where are you from?"

While Eli keeps Daisy occupied, Miles and Kai creep around behind the sofa. I notice Kai's hand dig into Daisy's purse, but she's too preoccupied with Eli to pay any attention. Miles quickly snaps a picture of her driver's license before stuffing her wallet back in her purse.

Damn. They're good. My brothers are the best. They're pains in my ass, cause me more heartburn and hangovers than should be allowed, but they're always there for me.

"Where's Adele?" Jaxon asks and all conversation and movement in the room halts.

"Yes." Daisy stands. "Where is she? I need to be going."

I stand with a sigh. "I'm sorry, Daisy. You won't be going anywhere with Adele."

"But she's my baby."

"Who you abandoned."

"She's mine!"

"Maybe I should call the lawyer." Eli digs his phone out of his pocket.

Daisy pales. "Your lawyer?"

Eli's brow wrinkles. "Didn't you tell her you're suing for custody?"

"I-I-I thought you were bluffing," Daisy stutters.

I cross my arms over my chest. "I'm serious. I am not letting you take Adele away from me."

She throws her arms in the air. "You didn't even want her."

I growl. "You arrived at my house with a baby I didn't know about. You didn't explain yourself. You barely told me her name before you fled. How did you think I'd react?"

"I didn't think you'd hire lawyers and sue me!"

Eli clears his throat. "We can forget about the lawyers. You can surrender Adele."

"Surrender Adele?" Daisy slaps a hand over her chest. "She's mine."

"Wrong," I growl. "She's mine."

"This was a wasted trip," she grumbles. "You could have let me know you were suing for custody before I traveled all the way here."

"I didn't know your last name or where you lived. How the hell was I supposed to contact you?"

She rolls her eyes. "It's not my fault you sleep with women without getting to know anything about them."

I swallow. She's right. I never should have had sex with her without knowing more about her. I was so busy trying not to become my dad that I became someone I didn't want to be.

Those days are over. Sloane is the only woman I'm interested in now. And forever if she'll have me. My stomach falls. After this scene with Daisy, she may give up on me completely.

"I think it's time for you to leave." Rhett herds her toward the door. He opens it and ushers her out. "I'll follow her to make sure she doesn't stay on the island."

I nod my thanks to him. Rhett is the family's protector. Daisy won't hurt me or Adele if he can help it.

"Where's Adele?" Kai asks.

"Here she is." Sloane enters, cradling my daughter. "I kept her in the nursery until Daisy left."

"Thank you." I gather Adele in my arms and Sloane stiffens.

Shit. After the scene with Daisy, I'm back to square one with her.

Chapter 24

"Note to self: teach Boozer the difference between a Christmas tree and a bathroom."

SLOANE

I wait until the door closes behind Daisy – no way was I allowing Adele to be in the presence of that woman any longer than necessary – before leaving the nursery.

"Where's Adele?" Kai asks.

"Here she is," I say. "I kept her in the nursery until she left."

"Thank you." Zane gathers Adele into his arms.

The love he has for his daughter is clear to see on his face. It only makes him sexier, which I would have said was impossible a few weeks ago.

"Does this mean you're filing for custody?" Eli asks.

"Hell, yeah, I am. I'm not letting anyone take Adele from me."

I love how fiercely he protects his daughter. How deeply he loves her. I want him to love me and be fiercely protective of me.

I stiffen. I don't want Zane – the player – to love me. How silly. I don't love him. Why would I want him to love me?

Liar. You're falling in love with him.

I want to deny it, but after watching Zane square off with Daisy to protect Adele, it's undeniable. I am falling for Zane.

Shit. These feelings can only lead to heartbreak. Zane may be ready to be a dad, but he hasn't changed his standpoint on relationships.

"Okay," Eli says and I startle. I forgot I was standing in a room with the Raider brothers. Great time to have an epiphany.

I inch backwards until I'm in the kitchen. Boozer follows me. He stands at the door to the yard wagging his tail. Good idea. I'll take him for a walk and clear my mind.

We slip outside. I wait a few moments, but when no one comes after us, I make my way around the house and down the street.

Boozer barks and tugs on his leash when he notices the neighbor, Addy, dragging her Christmas tree toward a cart parked in the middle of the street.

"Boozer, no!"

My shout seems to incite him as he breaks free and dashes to the Christmas tree. Addy shrieks and drops the tree. Boozer promptly lifts his leg and pees on it.

"Stop!"

I swear, if dogs could roll their eyes, he'd be rolling his eyes at me now.

"Sorry, Addy." I snatch Boozer's leash from the ground and yank him back.

Addy clutches his chest. "He scared me, is all. I didn't notice you walking him." She glances around. "Where's Zane and Adele? I want cuddles."

I ignore her question. I don't want to discuss Zane or Adele now. "What's happening?" I motion to the wagon filled with Christmas trees.

"The neighbors got together and rented a cart to bring our Christmas trees to the beach for the Smugglers' Blaze."

The Smugglers' Blaze is a New Year's Eve bonfire on the beach. The inhabitants of the island gather around and drink moonshine while saying goodbye to the year. I'm usually there working since *Rumrunner* has a booth selling drinks. Until the crowd gets too rowdy. Then, Harper shuts us down.

Addy narrows her eyes at me. "And don't think I didn't realize you changed the subject."

I shrug. "What is there to say? I'm out walking my dog. Adele and Zane aren't with me."

"Hmmm… You two have been getting quite close since you've been living with him."

I roll my eyes. "I'm the nanny. Of course, I live with him."

"Uh huh. Live with him."

"Since when are you into small town gossip?"

"Since I live on the same street as the current talk of the town."

"Whatever," I mumble. "I need to walk my dog."

My dog that is currently rolling around in the Christmas tree where he peed. Great. Someone's getting a bath today.

I tighten his leash and Boozer whines before giving up the Christmas tree. We don't make it another block before my phone rings. Geez. Can't a woman get an hour to sort herself after realizing she's falling for her boss? The player who will never settle down.

"Hey, Harper." Speaking of bosses.

"Where are you?"

"I'm walking my dog. What's wrong? Do you need me to come into work?"

The last thing I want to do is work on my day off. But maybe work will get my mind off of things.

"No."

"What's up?" In other words, why is she calling? Harper and I have been working together for years. We're friendly, but we're not exactly friends. Although, she didn't have much time for friends until recently.

"I …um… never mind." She hangs up and I stare at my phone. What just happened?

"There you are!" Dakota shouts from behind me.

I glance over my shoulder. She's rushing toward me. When she reaches me, she bends over and gasps for breath.

"Were you out jogging?"

"Yeah. Sure. Out jogging," she wheezes.

"While wearing jeans and boots?"

She finally catches her breath and stands. "Enough about me. Let's go have lunch." She threads her arm through mine.

"Lunch?"

I know Dakota. She comes into *Rumrunner* with her boyfriend, Rhett, whenever the Raider brothers get together. But we're not friends. Don't get me wrong. I like her. We just haven't had the chance to bond yet.

"It's the meal in between breakfast and dinner."

I snort. "I'm aware."

"Oh, look. What a lovely surprise. Blossom and Harper are here, too." She motions to the two women hurrying toward us.

"Who's ready for lunch?" Blossom asks when she joins us.

"I'm starving," Harper adds.

I skid to a halt. "What is going on?"

"I'm going to tell her," Harper declares.

I narrow my eyes. "Tell me what? What's going on? Is Adele hurt?" I try to turn around and head back to the house but Harper stops me.

"Adele is fine." She squeezes my arm before releasing mine. "Everyone is fine."

"More than fine." Dakota winks.

Blossom groans. "Please, don't wink. Whenever you wink, you forget how to walk and bump into someone. Usually a big someone who thinks you're coming on to him. It never ends well."

Dakota glares at her. "I can walk and wink at the same time."

Blossom snorts. "Sure, you can."

"Ladies." Harper claps to get everyone's attention. "Can we get back to the matter at hand?"

"Which is?" I ask.

"We're having lunch with you while the men meet with the lawyer about Adele's custody," Blossom says.

"Wow. Zane didn't wait long to get the ball rolling."

"Is there another area Zane has been waiting on?" Blossom asks.

"What are you…" I trail off when I realize what she's insinuating. "Zane and I aren't a couple. I'm the nanny. End of discussion."

"Come on." Harper herds us forward. "Let's discuss this over a burger at the *Salty Siren.* Just don't tell my dad I had an unhealthy burger. He'll lose his mind."

"And no stopping to play games on the boardwalk," Blossom adds. "Someone," she points to Dakota, "is banned from the games."

"I'm not banned," Dakota declares. Blossom raises her eyebrows. "I was strongly advised not to return. It's not the same as banned."

"Paisely apologizes," Harper says as we wander toward the boardwalk.

"About what?"

"Stephanie isn't feeling well. She had to skip the Raider sisters' lunch."

"Raider sisters?"

Dakota's nose wrinkles. "You don't approve of the name?"

"I don't understand the name. As far as I know, there are only Raider brothers."

"And their wives and girlfriends and fiancées."

I screech to a halt. "I'm not a wife, girlfriend, or fiancée of a Raider brother."

"Not yet," Dakota sings as she threads her arm through mine.

I decide not to argue with her. For some reason, these women have decided I'm one of them. As much as I'd love to be one of them – I want to have a family more than anything in the world – I'm not. Zane is my boss, the father of the baby I'm helping to care for.

No matter how much I may wish for more, he doesn't feel the same. And attaching myself to these women who are intimately connected to Zane's brothers isn't a good idea. When I'm no longer Zane's nanny, it'll be too painful to have friends who are part of his life when I no longer am.

"I just remembered. I have Boozer. He's not allowed in the *Salty Siren.*"

Dakota waves a hand in dismissal. "Don't worry. They let my dog, Delphine, in there all the time."

"Your dog doesn't try to steal burgers out of people's mouths."

As if he knows what I'm saying, Boozer barks.

"If a smuggler doesn't know better than to let a dog steal their burger, it's their own fault."

Harper's correct. Smugglers do know better. Considering the amount of pranks pulled on this island, inhabitants are well aware of the need to protect their food.

"Boozer can't go through Smuggler's Market. He'll wreak destruction."

Smuggler's Market is a craft fair on the boulevard. During the summer, the market is every weekend. But in the off-season, the market only happens around holidays or festivals.

"We can…" Harper trails off.

"We can what?"

She nods to something behind me and I whirl around to find Zane stalking toward us. He appears mad. Why is he mad? Did things not go well at the lawyer's?

"Did you fucking run away from me?"

I rear back. "Are you mad at me?"

Dakota snatches Boozer's leash from me. "I'll bring him back tomorrow."

I don't have a chance to protest before she rushes off with my dog. Blossom and Harper trail after her.

I focus my attention on Zane. His jaw is clenched, and his nostrils are flaring. He's not mad. He's pissed.

"What's wrong?"

Chapter 25

"She says I don't know her. Funny, I know exactly how she sounds when she comes."

ZANE

What's wrong? Is she seriously asking me what's wrong, as if she didn't run away from me? What the fuck?

"We'll discuss this at home."

I capture her wrist and start for home.

"It's not my home," she mutters.

"Are you fucking kidding me? You live there. It's your home."

"Only until I can find somewhere else to live."

"Are you…"

I trail off when I realize there are several people listening to our conversation. I notice one or two reach for their phones. I do not want to be the talk of the town. And I don't want Sloane to be embarrassed.

"We'll discuss this at *home*." I emphasize the word home. I'll keep emphasizing it until Sloane realizes my house is exactly where she belongs. My house with me. And my daughter. Our little family.

We arrive home within minutes. It's a good thing the walk wasn't long, as my anger grew with each step we took.

"Where's Adele?"

"She's at my mom's while we sort this out."

"Sort what out?"

"Why you ran away."

"I didn't run away. I was walking my dog."

I stalk toward her and she retreats until her back hits the living room wall. I slam my hands on the wall, caging her in.

"You didn't tell me you were leaving. My brothers were all here and you snuck out the back door."

"I didn't want to bother you."

"Stop lying to me," I grit out.

"I'm not lying."

I inhale a deep breath and get my temper under control. Being mad at her is not helping things.

"Sweetness." I tuck a strand of hair behind her ear and palm her neck. "I know you. I know when you're lying."

"You don't know me."

"I know you always glance to the left when you lie."

"I do not."

"You're doing it now."

She huffs. "Well, give Mr. Raider a cookie. He knows my tell."

"I know more than your tell. I know how much your mom hurts you when she's dismissive of you and your life. I know you long for a family. I know you're keeping your distance from me because you're afraid I'm the same as your dad."

She gasps, and her jaw drops open.

I chuckle and use a finger to lift her chin to close her mouth. "What did you think? I didn't pay any attention to you?" I lean close to whisper in her ear. "I've had my mouth on you. I've tasted your sweetness. I know how you sound when you come."

Her eyes flare and her breath hitches. "You're not playing fair."

"Never said I would. Now, tell me. Why did you run away?"

"I…" She glances to the left and I growl. "I don't want to tell you."

At least she's being honest. "Why not?"

"It's private."

I should respect her privacy, but I can't. Her reason for running away involves me. I know it does.

"I guess I'll have to tease the truth out of you."

"Tease?"

I press my hard length into her belly. "Tease."

"How are you hard right now?"

"I have the woman I want in my arms. Of course, I'm hard." I'm not telling her she's the woman I love. She'll run straight into the ocean, screaming for the mermaids to adopt her if I utter those words.

"The woman you want?"

"Why are you confused? I've made it perfectly obvious I want you."

"We never discussed what happened. I assumed…"

"You assumed?"

"I was merely a body for you to use."

I growl. "You are not merely a body to me. Did it feel like I was using you when I had my mouth on you?"

"No."

"Does it feel like I'm using you now? After I spent an hour driving all over the island to find you. I had to activate the Raider family tree to search for you."

"I wasn't gone an hour. I would have come back eventually."

"I wasn't waiting for you to return. I wasn't leaving you out there alone to stew on whatever's bothering you."

She practically melts in my arms. "You weren't?"

"Nope. Now are you ready to tell me what's bothering you?"

She studies me for a moment before shaking her head.

"I guess I'm teasing it out of you." Her eyes flare, but I need her verbal confirmation before I go any further. "If you don't want me to touch every inch of you, to taste every inch of you, to bury myself deep inside you, say the word now and I'll walk away."

"You'd walk away?"

"Yes."

"But you're hard."

"Doesn't matter. I need your consent before I proceed. Do I have it?" She bites her bottom lip. I wait. Finally, she nods. "I need your words."

"Yes, Zane. I'm saying yes."

"Thank, fuck," I mutter before throwing her over my shoulder and carrying her into my bedroom. I dump her on my bed and scowl.

"What's wrong? Did you change your mind?" She inches toward the edge of the bed but I stop her with a hand on her leg.

"I did not change my mind. I just realized I need to buy a new mattress and bedding."

"What? You're thinking about mattresses and bedding?"

I don't want to fuck her on the same mattress I fucked other women on. Sloane is special. She's my end game. She deserves more.

But I'm not discussing other women with her. She's skittish enough. Considering her father, I don't blame her.

"Never mind. I'm an idiot."

She giggles. "You said it."

I lay on top of her. "Are you making fun of me?" I tickle her ribs and she bats my hands away.

I grasp her hands and place them above her head. "Hands on the headboard."

"Why?" she questions, but she does as I ask.

"So, I can do this."

I grasp the hem of her sweater and pull it off. I throw it over my shoulder.

"I love this lacey number." I trace a finger along the edge of her bra. Her breasts strain against the material. "But it has to go, too."

I flick open her bra. "Gorgeous."

I massage and plump her breasts. Her nipples harden but I don't touch them.

"Please."

"Please, what?" I ask.

"Touch me."

"I am touching you."

She grunts and I tuck my chin to hide my grin.

"You know what I want."

"And you know what I want. Are you ready to give it to me?" My hands still as I wait for her answer.

"You don't own me. I'm allowed to have private thoughts."

Someone's stubborn. I'll tease the answer out of her eventually. I blow air over her breast and watch as her nipple tightens further. She moans and thrusts her chest into my face. Who am I to deny her?

I lick and nibble her flesh until she's writhing beneath me. I latch onto her nipple and she moans hard and long.

I continue to tease her nipple with my teeth and tongue while my hand massages her other breast. She wraps her legs around my waist and rubs her core against my cock.

I still.

"Why are you stopping? Don't stop. I didn't tell you to stop."

I push her legs off me. "You are not getting yourself off by rubbing against me."

"You're too slow."

"Are you ready to tell me why you ran?"

She scowls. "No."

I sigh. "Too bad. I was having fun."

I get to my knees. She opens her mouth to complain but I press my finger against her lips. "Unless you're telling me why you ran or moaning my name, I don't want to hear it."

She glares at me.

"I promise to sink deep inside you and give you at least two orgasms if you confess."

Her eyes narrow. I guess she's not ready to share yet.

I glide my fingers down her body until I reach her jeans. I don't waste any more time. I unsnap her jeans and slide her zipper down.

"Up," I order.

She lifts her ass and I drag her jeans and panties down her legs. She's now gloriously naked for me. I pause a moment to memorize how beautiful she is. Her face is flushed, and her chest is heaving. Damn. She's glorious. I can't wait to watch her face when she climaxes.

I stand. As quick as I can, I remove my clothes. Sloane bites her lip. To her credit, she doesn't speak.

I grab a condom from my bedside drawer and don it.

When I crawl back onto the bed, she opens her legs to accommodate me. "Are you ready to confess yet?"

She shakes her head.

I draw my hands up her legs. How does she get her skin this smooth? Is it her lotion that smells of strawberries?

I avoid her clit and go straight for her pussy. I sink two fingers inside and her walls convulse around me. I plunge in and out of her until her walls shake and tighten around me.

She's close to coming, but I'm not letting her come until she tells me why she ran.

I remove my fingers and she scowls at me.

"Ready to confess yet?"

She glares at me. "You're an asshole."

"I'm an asshole who was worried sick when you disappeared."

"Fine. I was scared. Are you happy now?"

Not yet. But I will be soon. We both will be. "Why were you scared?"

"I realized how much I want you and it scared me."

My heart hammers against my chest. This woman I love wants me. I knew she wanted me. We're in this bed together after all. But she's frightened of how much? This can only mean one thing – she cares for me.

Good. This is a start. I'll get her to fall in love with me. But first, I'm going to show her how much she means to me.

"Hold onto the headboard," I grumble.

"Why?"

"Because I'm going to fuck you now."

She lifts her hands and I notch my cock at her entrance.

"Hold on," I demand before slamming into her.

Fuck. Fuck. Fuck. My balls are heavy and my lower back tingles. I'm ready to come, and all I did was bury myself inside her.

Her walls ripple around me and I grit my teeth. I refuse to be a one-pump wonder. Not when I'm trying to show this woman how much I care for her.

I inhale a deep breath to get myself under control. And then I go about showing Sloane how much she means to me.

Chapter 26

"Apparently, sarcasm isn't an effective shield. Who knew?"

SLOANE

The arm around my waist tightens and I groan. Stupid sexy smugglers. I did it again. I let Zane have his wicked way with me.

Am I an idiot? Or worse yet – am I my mother? Why can't I resist Zane?

I know he's not interested in a relationship. He may have changed his tune about being a father, but he's still a player. My dad wouldn't stay for me. Why would Zane?

I need to get out of here. I lift his arm and scoot toward the edge of the bed.

"Where do you think you're going?"

"Bathroom."

"Come straight back to me."

I nod. It's not lying if I nod.

I snag my clothes from the floor before rushing from the room. When I reach the bathroom, I lock the door behind me and lean against it. I slide to the floor.

Why did I give in and have sex with Zane again?

Because you're falling in love with him.

True, but he's not in love with me. He doesn't even want a relationship with me. Sleeping with him will tether me tighter to him, but it won't affect him. I need to keep my distance.

Starting now. I quickly do my business and don my clothes.

But when I open the bathroom door – intent on fleeing the house – Zane is there. He's leaning against the wall with his arms crossed over his bare chest. Too bad he put sweats on. I wouldn't mind one last chance to memorize his body.

"Where do you think you're going?"

"I need to pick up Boozer." I nearly pat myself on the back. Excellent excuse, Sloane.

"You can pick up Boozer after we talk."

I nearly shiver at the demand in his voice. It's the same voice he uses when he's giving orders in bed. Orders, I'm happy to follow since Zane knows how to make a woman feel good. I guess practice does make perfect.

At the reminder of just how much practice he's had, I scowl. Players are always going to play.

"Scowl all you want. This conversation is happening."

Zane shackles my wrist and leads me toward the bedroom. I plant my feet.

"I'm not having a conversation without coffee."

He pivots toward the kitchen without saying a word. When we reach the table, he pushes me down in a chair. "Sit. I'll make the coffee."

"I'm perfectly capable of making my own coffee."

"Are you going to argue about every-damn-thing this morning?"

I shrug since it's quite possible I will argue about everything this morning. Especially if this 'talk' will result in me losing my position as his nanny and being kicked out of his home.

My stomach falls. I didn't think this through. I never should have had sex with the man I'm working for and living with. Could I be more stupid? Have I learned nothing from my mom and how I grew up? Bouncing from house to house as she switched from boyfriend to boyfriend.

Zane kneels in front of me and clasps my hands. "Just breathe, sweetness."

"I am breathing."

"There's no reason to panic."

"Ha! Easy for you to say. You're not the one who's going to be kicked out of the place where she lives today. I don't want to live in my car again. It's cold and scary and loud. I guess I can stay in a hotel for a few nights. Shit. It's New Year's Eve. I'll never find a hotel room tonight. They're booked up months in advance on Smuggler's Hideaway. Even the *Mermaid Motel* is fully booked this time of year. I can't exactly crash with—"

Zane places his finger over my lips. "I'm not kicking you out."

I slap his finger away. "But we had sex. This is what you do. You have sex and kick the woman out the next morning."

He growls. "You aren't some woman I picked up in a bar." I open my mouth to respond but he snaps at me. "I'm speaking now."

I motion for him to continue.

"I don't sleep with women. I don't cuddle women all night long. Only you."

A tiny spark of hope ignites in me. Is he serious? Am I different?

"Why am I different? It's not as if you're going to suddenly decide, 'Hey! I'm no longer terrified of relationships.'"

He clears his throat. "Actually, I am."

My mouth drops open. "W-w-what?"

"And, technically, I was never terrified of relationships."

"Says the man whose face used to turn green if someone uttered the word."

"I wasn't terrified of relationships. I was afraid of becoming my father."

I get it. I don't want to become my mother either. Except here I am falling in love with a player. Goal not achieved. Go back to start.

"But you showed me I'm not my father. I didn't abandon Adele when she needed me. And I'm not giving her back to her mother now. She had her chance. She blew it. Adele is mine now."

I bite back a sigh. When Zane speaks about his daughter, it's impossible not to fall for him. He's possessive of her, and the love he has for her is boundless.

"You're a good father."

"Thank you. And thank you for helping me find my way."

I shrug. "You would have found your way without me. You have this great big family ready and willing to help you."

The Raider family is everything I've ever wanted. They're loud, love to pull pranks, and cause trouble wherever they go. But they're also supportive and rush to each other's aid at the first sign of trouble.

Spending Christmas morning with them was glorious. I want to spend all my holidays with them. I want to spend all of my days with this man kneeling before me.

But dreams don't come true for women like me. My mom taught me that lesson over and over again.

"We're getting off track," Zane says and I focus on him. He smiles and his blue eyes sparkle while the dimples on his left cheek appear. To say he's gorgeous is a massive understatement.

"What track are we supposed to be on?"

"The track where we decide we're in a relationship."

I feign cleaning my ears. "Sorry. I think my ears are plugged."

He rolls his eyes. "You heard me, but I don't have a problem repeating myself. We're in a relationship now."

"And you decided this all by yourself. You don't think maybe I should have a say in it?"

"You had a say when you told me you care for me."

I purse my lips. "I never said I care for you."

It's true, but I didn't say it. I was very careful not to.

He shrugs. "You're scared of how big your feelings are for me. Same thing."

I narrow my eyes at him. "I didn't say I was scared of how big my feelings are for you."

He sighs. "Yes, you did. Do I have to tease the truth out of you again?"

My nipples tingle. I like this idea. Way too much.

"Maybe?"

"Fine. But we don't have as much time as last night. I miss our baby girl. We both have the day off. I want to spend the day with our little family."

Forget about the nipples. My heart is pounding in my chest. *Our baby girl. Our little family.* He can't be serious. I clutch my chest to stop my heart from escaping.

"Sweetness." Zane places his hands on my cheeks and I meet his gaze. "I don't know why you're shocked. I told you we're in a relationship now."

"You can't make a one-sided decision," I snap.

"Fine. Sloane Wilder, do you want to date me? Do you want to be in a relationship with me?"

I do, but I can't risk it. He's a player. He won't stay.

He growls. "Do not compare me with your dad. I am not that asshole who abandoned you before you were born."

"I didn't mention my dad."

He taps my temple. "You were thinking of him."

"This knowing all my tells thing sucks," I mutter.

He smirks. "You don't enjoy how I know which parts of your body to touch to make you squirm? To get you all hot and bothered?"

My breath hitches. I enjoy it entirely too much. It's what got me into this mess in the first place.

He leans his forehead against mine. "Give me a chance, Sloane. I promise I'll make it worth your while. I'll also screw up. Probably a lot."

I nibble on my lip. I want to say yes. Badly. This is the man I'm falling in love with. Oh, who am I kidding? The second he said 'our little family', I was a goner. How could I not love this man who wants to give me what I've never had but want the most?

"I don't know."

"I promise I won't be your dad. I won't abandon you."

"But if everything falls apart, I not only lose you, I lose Adele." I'll lose what little family I have.

"I will work my ass off to avoid that conclusion. I know you want this, sweetness. I know you're scared. I'm scared, too. But I won't let my fear stop me from getting what I want."

My muscles tighten with the need to flee. To avoid the heartbreak he can cause. But isn't fleeing every time things got tough exactly what my mom did? She always left her boyfriends when she thought they weren't paying enough attention to her or weren't enamored with her anymore.

I straighten my shoulders. I will not be my mom.

"Okay."

Zane grins. "Okay?"

I nod. "I want to be in a relationship with you."

He presses his lips against mine in a hard, quick kiss. "I want to kiss the shit out of you right now, but I won't be able to stop there. And I really miss Adele. Let's spend the day together."

He stands and offers me his hand. This time, I don't hesitate to take it.

This decision might lead me to heartache, but at least I'll have tried.

Chapter 27

"I wanted a nursery. But I think I need a bigger house."

ZANE

I roll over and reach for Sloane but encounter cold, empty sheets instead. I grunt. I want to wake up to her in my arms every day.

Sloane had other ideas. She thinks we should slow things down. She doesn't trust my feelings yet, but she will. In the meantime, she's sleeping in the guest bedroom down the hall.

"Wah."

Adele's awake. I quickly dress and use the bathroom before making my way to the nursery.

I frown at all of the boxes filling up the space. This isn't a nursery. This is a storage space with a crib and a changing table. It appears temporary. As if I'm not prepared to keep Adele.

The custody trial is next week. What if the court decides they want a home visit? The judge will never believe I'm serious about my daughter if she sees this.

Sloane stumbles into the room thirty minutes later. Her eyes widen at the mess I've created.

"What are you doing?"

"I'm getting rid of all the boxes."

She pushes her hair out of her face. "Why?"

"This room wasn't a nursery. It was a storage space."

"It wasn't too bad. All of the boxes were piled up against the one corner."

I scowl. "Not good enough."

"Zane, what's going on? You didn't have a problem with this setup yesterday."

"Yesterday, I didn't know the judge from the custody hearing can stop by for a visit to ascertain whether the house is good enough for my baby girl."

I reach for the next box but she steps in my way to stop me. "You're worried about the custody hearing?"

I thread my hands through my hair and pull on the ends. "Of course, I'm worried. Some judge I don't know can decide I'm not good enough to be a father."

She wraps her arms around me. "You're good enough. You're a great father."

"A judge doesn't know that. They'll take one look at this room and think I don't care for Adele."

"Bullsh—" Her eyes catch on Adele playing in her bouncer and she cuts herself off. "Wrong. It's plain to see how much you love your daughter."

I drop my chin to my chest and enfold Sloane in my arms. "Maybe I should let Daisy have Adele. Babies should be with their mothers."

Sloane glares up at me. "Daisy is no more a fit mom for Adele than my mom was for me."

She's right. The way Daisy abandoned my girl…I blow out a breath. "I know. I'm just worried."

"You can be worried. This is a big deal, and it's scary. But I will not allow you for one second to think Adele would be better off with Daisy."

My lips twitch. "You won't allow it?"

"You heard me, buster." She pokes me. "I won't allow it."

I grin at her. "Thank you."

"Why are you thanking me?"

"For calming me down."

"You never have to thank me for calming you down. You thanking me would mean I have to thank you whenever you calm me down, and let's face it, no one has time for the amount of thanking that would be necessary."

I bark out a laugh. Adele giggles in response.

Sloane smiles before pulling out of my arms to go to my baby girl. She picks her up from her bouncer.

"Good morning, sweetie pie. How are you this morning?" Adele gurgles. "You are going to break all the boys' hearts."

I growl. No boy is going to get near my baby girl. "Adele will not be dating until she's thirty."

"Daddy is crazy, isn't he?" Sloane coos to Adele.

Adele claps her hands. "Ba-ba!"

"Can you say da-da?"

"Ba-ba!"

I watch the woman I love with my baby girl, and I know I made the right decision to keep them both. I will not let anyone take either one of them away from me. I will fight to the bitter end for my girls.

Adele launches herself at me and I catch her. I will always catch her. Whatever she wants, she can have. Including a nursery.

"Can you watch her while I deal with these boxes?"

"Why don't you call your brothers? You'll have the boxes emptied and the contents squared away in no time with their help."

"It's New Year's Day. I don't want to disturb them."

She checks the time. "It's only nine. The Salty Dip doesn't start until noon."

"And last night was New Year's Eve. My brothers were probably at the Smugglers' Blaze until it closed down."

"Wrong. Eli and Rhett left when you did. They wanted to get their families home. Jaxon used the excuse to sneak away since the activity was no longer a Raider brother activity. Whatever that means. Miles snuck off about an hour after they did. No idea where he went."

"Did you notice Hazel around? If she's around, you'll find Miles mooning over her."

She rolls her eyes. "Only Kai and Harper stayed until the end because they were helping me at the booth."

I frown. "I hate that you had to work all night and I wasn't there."

Her brow wrinkles. "This is what I do. I'm a bartender. I usually work all night."

"Harper gave you the night off."

"She needed help. I wasn't letting her and Kai work the booth on their own. Truth be told." She pauses to yawn. "We could have used at least two more bartenders. The lines were obnoxious. Kai had to run to *Rumrunner* for another case of moonshine at one point."

I can't argue with her. Sloane is loyal. She'd never abandon anyone who needed help. Thus, her becoming my nanny even when she didn't trust me.

"Go ahead and ring your brothers. I'll deal with Adele."

Deal with Adele? I glance down and notice how her face is straining. Uh oh. This is her poop face. I don't hesitate to hand her off to Sloane.

"You still hate changing poopy diapers."

"I'll get used to it by the time we have our third child."

She gasps. "Third child?"

I'm not about to tell her I want to give her the family she's always longed for. She's still getting used to the idea of us and wants to take things slow.

I do the only thing I can think of. I hurry out of the room.

Eli, Jaxon, and Rhett arrive within thirty minutes. Kai begged off since Harper's dad is having a bad day. He had a stroke some years ago and struggles with mobility. And I couldn't reach Miles. I hope he's not somewhere making bad decisions.

"What's happening? What do you need?" Eli asks when we gather in the living room.

"The nursery. It's a bit of a mess."

Rhett grins. "Dakota has been dying to get her hands on your nursery for weeks. I'll phone her."

"I can watch Pearl and Mira," Sloane offers.

"Thanks, sis." Rhett strolls out of the room with his phone to his ear.

Sloane stares after him. I squeeze her hand. "You're part of this family, sweetness," I whisper to her. She smiles up at me and I can't resist. I meld my lips to hers.

"Hell yeah!" Eli shouts and I tear myself away from Sloane to glare at him.

"You can't be mad at me for being happy for you."

"I can be mad if you've been making bets about us and are happy because you won."

Before Eli can respond, Rhett strolls back into the room. "Dakota's on her way with the kids. And Mom will be here in an hour with lunch."

Jaxon fiddles with his glasses. "I'm uncertain why I'm here."

"I figured you could put the bookshelf and cupboard together faster than anyone else." I shrug. "I guess I was wrong."

Jaxon narrows his eyes. "You're not wrong."

Sloane smirks. "I have an idea. Why don't we have a little competition? Jaxon can put the bookshelf together while Eli does the cupboard. Whoever loses has to babysit Adele on five different occasions."

"No fair. A bookshelf is way easier to put together than a cupboard," Eli claims.

"Not for me. I'm in. I'll put the cupboard together faster than you can do the bookshelf. Unless you're too scared?" Jaxon raises an eyebrow.

Eli glares at him. "You're on."

They shake hands before sprinting to the nursery. "Hold on," Sloane chases after them. "We need rules."

Rhett barks out a laugh. "Rules? Sloane should know better than to impose rules on Raiders."

He's wrong since when Sloane returns with Jaxon and Eli, they're nodding in agreement to whatever she's saying while they each carry a large box.

"I'll get my toolbox."

By the time I return from the garage, the furniture has been moved out of the way. I set the toolbox in between the two large boxes before backing away. I don't want to be anywhere near Eli or Jaxon when they begin.

"Ready! Set! Go!"

As soon as Sloane says go, they break into the boxes. The door opens and Dakota enters with Pearl and Mira.

"Unka Eli!" Pearl shouts and rushes to him.

Sloane scoops her up before she reaches him. "Do you want to play with me this morning?"

"Mom! I'm going to play with Aunt Sloane."

Sloane's eyes well with tears. But she sucks them up and smiles at Pearl. "What do you want to do first?"

I watch as they walk toward Sloane's bedroom. I know I'm going to screw up with her a lot. One thing I did right, though, is to give her a family. I can't repair her relationship with her mom or find her dad, but I can share my brothers and their partners with her.

And I can give her children. I already consider Adele hers but she needs more children. A big family is what she's always wanted and I'm ready to give it to her.

I need a bigger house.

Chapter 28

"Sometimes love feels like riding a carousel with smugglers yelling sea monster noises."

SLOANE

I check my phone for the tenth time in the last minute. Still no news from Zane.

This morning is the custody hearing. I wanted to go with him to show my support but Zane's lawyer, Siena, cautioned against it. She's seen things get nasty at a hearing when a new partner shows up.

I didn't want to, but I accepted her advice. I won't do anything to jeopardize Zane's chances of keeping Adele.

Usually, I spend my mornings caring for Adele while Zane is at work, but there was no way I could stay home with nothing to do this morning. Which is why I'm currently in the storage room at *Rumrunner* doing inventory.

Harper pats my hand. "It'll be okay. No one's taking Zane's baby from him."

I blow out a breath. "The waiting is killing me. I want to be there with him. Supporting him. I'm failing at being in a relationship."

"You're not failing. You're giving him what he needs."

"I never knew you were good at pep talks."

She shrugs. "I never had time for pep talks before Kai."

Her love for him shines from her. She fought Kai long and hard – he's eight years younger than her, which was a no go for her – but he wouldn't give up. He kept pushing and pushing until she finally gave in. They're now engaged to be married.

"I'm happy for you."

"And I'm happy for you."

"Whoa." I hold up a hand. "Don't jump the gun. Zane and I have barely started dating."

"Zane's never dated before. But he changed his ways. For you."

I wave her comment away. I have enough worries at the moment. I'm not adding worrying about Zane returning to his playboy ways to the list.

"I wish he'd call."

"Come on." She drops her clipboard on a shelf. "Why don't I show you how to use the HR management software."

My eyes widen. "The HR management software?"

"You'll need to know how to use it when you're the assistant manager."

Excitement bubbles through me. Assistant manager is the position I've been angling for. Harper's been reluctant to promote me because I might have had time management issues in the past.

I've been trying to prove to her I've changed. That I can handle the extra responsibility. That she can rely on me.

My hard work is paying off.

"Okay. Let's do this."

I follow her to the office and sit next to her behind her computer. "It's pretty intuitive, but if you get stuck, there are videos online to help."

She shows me how to log in to the software before giving me a tour of the features. There's recruiting, onboarding, time and attendance tracking, performance reviews, benefits administration, and payroll. It's a lot more than I expected.

She's showing me how to log someone's hours when the back entrance of the bar bangs open. Zane charges into the office a few seconds later.

"Zane!" I rush to him. "What happened? Did you get custody?" I glance behind him. "Where's Adele?"

"Adele is in the car with Mom. I insisted we stop here before going home."

"What happened?"

"She didn't show. Daisy didn't fucking show up to a custody hearing for her own child."

"This is good, right? You'll definitely get custody now."

He purses his lips. "Siena says it isn't a given. The judge still needs to ensure I'm a fit father. And this judge leans heavily toward mothers keeping their children."

"What a bunch of malarky! Daisy abandoned Adele and didn't even show up to the custody hearing. She shouldn't get visitation rights. Let alone custody!"

"I'm trying to comfort myself with those thoughts, but Siena said I shouldn't get my hopes up." He threads his hands through his hair and pulls.

I'm a horrible partner. Here, Zane is worried he's going to lose his child, and I'm getting all riled up about what a bitch Daisy is. I should be supporting him. Not adding to his problems.

I grasp his hand and squeeze. "Did Siena indicate when you'll hear from the judge?"

"It could be a few days or a few weeks."

"I'm certain the judge will side with you. Were you able to give evidence about how you've been caring for Adele for the past two months?"

He nods. "Even though Daisy didn't show, the judge asked us to present our case."

He tears away from me to pace the office. Harper isn't behind her desk. She must have slipped out and I didn't realize.

"I don't know what I'll do if they take my baby girl from me."

Distraction. He needs a distraction. Otherwise, he'll spend the entire day worrying about the custody hearing. There's nothing he can do about it now anyway.

"Why don't we go on an outing with Adele?"

"An outing?"

"We can visit *Mermaid Mystical Gardens.* I bet she'd love it. We'll invite the whole family."

The theme park has plenty of rides for young children. If Adele is anything like her dad, she'll love it.

Harper peeks inside the office. "I'll contact everyone. We'll meet you there."

I grin at Zane. "I guess we're going."

We drive to the theme park with Zane's mom and stepdad. When we park and step out of the car, the Raider brothers are already arriving. This family can assemble quickly whenever fun is involved. His brothers and their partners join us at the entrance.

"What do you think of Zane's dad-mobile?" Miles asks.

My brow wrinkles. "What dad-mobile?"

He points to the car we arrived in.

"I thought it was your mom's car."

"Nope. It's Zane's dad-mobile."

"Did you sell your bike?" I ask Zane.

I hope he didn't sell his bike. I haven't gotten to ride on it yet. Mom had plenty of boyfriends who had bikes but I wasn't ever allowed on the back of them. Mom didn't care about my safety. She was worried about how much younger than her I was. In other words, she was jealous. Of her own daughter.

"No, but I needed a car for Adele," Zane explains. "I couldn't keep borrowing yours."

"Why not?"

"Because it's not big enough for more kids."

I gasp. "More kids?"

He chuckles. "When I plant my babies in you."

My knees wobble. He wants to have children with me? I love our little family, but I've always wanted a big family. Maybe not six boys. Smuggler's Hideaway can't survive a second generation of Raider brothers. But three or four children sounds good.

I notice Zane's brothers inching closer to us. Nosy little creepers.

I hold up a hand. "Zane Raider, you have lost your mind. We are not discussing this now."

"Let's go." Miles herds everyone toward the entrance. "I want to ride the *Atlantis Adventure* first."

"No way," Zane grumbles. "The last time we rode through the lost city of Atlantis, we nearly got kicked out."

"But we didn't," Miles sings.

"Only because I knew a secret exit," Paisley adds. "We should go on the *Enchanted Tide Carousel* first. Stephanie loves it."

The *Enchanted Tide Carousel* isn't your usual carousel ride. Instead of horses, zebras, and unicorns, the ride has mermaids, mermen, kraken, sirens, and other mythical sea creatures.

"Good idea. We can teach Adele all about mermaids," I say.

Zane laughs. "She's a bit young for sea lore."

"You're never too young for mermaids."

We make our way to the *Enchanted Tide Carousel.* "I'm not going on a carousel ride," Henry, Harper's dad, announces when we arrive.

"Good. You can guard the strollers."

Within seconds, the poor man is surrounded by strollers and diaper bags. "I didn't sign up for this. If anyone wants a free stroller, they can have it."

Stuart sits down next to him. "I'll help you guard the stuff."

"Help me?" Henry snorts. "You're on your own." He points to the wheelchair he's sitting in. "I can't exactly chase anyone with this thing. But the kids said I couldn't come if I didn't use it."

"Dad." Harper sighs. "Do we need to discuss how you sit down at the most random and inappropriate places when you get tired while using your cane?"

"I don't know what the big deal is."

Harper crosses her arms over her chest. "They had to close the drive-thru when you refused to move."

"Those cars could have driven around me."

She throws up her arms. "I give up."

Kai captures her hand and leads her to the line for the carousel. "He's giving you a hard time and you're letting him."

"Whose side are you on anyway?"

The previous ride ends and the attendant opens the gate for us. "Who wants to play sound charades?" Miles asks as he rushes to ride the kraken. "Winner picks the next ride."

"You're on!" Kai slaps Miles on his back as he passes him to mount a Scylla – a six-headed, twelve-legged monster.

Zane and I settle on a carriage towed by two hydras – multi-headed serpent-like beasts – with Adele settled in between us.

"What are the chances we get kicked off this ride?" I ask once the ride begins and the siren song begins playing.

"Woof! Woof!" Kai yelps from atop the Scylla.

"About twenty-five percent," Zane says.

Miles roars from atop the Kraken.

"Make that fifty percent," Zane mutters.

I burst into laughter. Life with Zane and his brothers is never boring. I can't wait to spend my life with the Raiders. Especially Zane. I love this man so much it scares me. But I'm no longer running from my fear. I'm throwing my arms in the air and enjoying the ride.

Come what may.

Chapter 29

"She thinks slow isn't in my vocabulary. Time to prove her wrong."

ZANE

My phone rings and I nearly push ignore before I notice who's calling. *Siena Kline.*

I've been waiting for my lawyer's call. It's been three days since the custody hearing. Three days of being too anxious to sleep. Three days of worrying about my baby girl being stolen from me. Three days of figuring out how to respond if the worst happens.

I start to answer but pause. I want to learn this news with Sloane by my side. I've leaned on her for the past days and she hasn't disappointed. She's been there for me every step of the way. I want her to be with me for this, too.

I push away from my desk. I'm going to Sloane.

I arrive at home within ten minutes. I love living in a small community where I don't have to spend hours driving in traffic or be crowded into a train with hundreds of other people.

Hold on. I've spent my life escaping Smuggler's Hideaway at every opportunity. And now I love it here? What changed?

The front door of the house opens and Sloane steps outside.

She's what's changed. Her and my baby girl. My family.

I never wanted a family before. I never wanted a relationship at all. But finding out I'm a father changed everything. And falling in love with Sloane made it even better.

"What's wrong?" Sloane asks when I reach the porch.

I kiss her quick. "Where's Adele?"

"Having a playdate with Stephanie. Eli said he'd bring her home after dinner."

I grasp her hand and pull her into the house.

"What is going on? Why are you home early?"

"My lawyer called."

She squeezes my hand. "And? What did she say?"

"I don't know."

She rears back. "You don't know? Did you black out while she was talking? Do we need the hospital? How many concussions have you had anyway? Should we get a CT scan of your brain?"

I wrap my arms around her. "There's nothing wrong with me. And Miles is the one who's had a ton of concussions."

She cuddles into me. "Why don't you know what the lawyer said?"

"I want to find out with you."

She smiles up at me. "You do?"

I cup her face. "Of course. You're the person who's standing beside me. Who's kept me sane for the past days. Who's raising Adele with me."

Her face softens. "I l—" She clears her throat. "Thank you."

I search her face. Was she about to confess her love to me? I hope to hell she loves me because I love this woman more than I thought was possible.

I dig my phone out of my pocket. "Let's do this."

I start to call Siena but I notice she left a voicemail. I push play.

"Hello, Zane. I heard from the judge in your custody hearing today. We'll receive the official papers soon, but he wanted me to know first. It's good news, Zane. Adele is yours. You have full custody. Daisy doesn't even have visitation rights. I'll call you tomorrow."

I clutch my chest as my heart threatens to burst out of it. "Adele is mine. She's mine."

"This is the best news. Let me phone the family."

I swipe Sloane's phone out of her hand. "No family. Not yet."

Her gaze clashes with mine. "Don't you want to celebrate?"

I herd her backwards. "Oh, we're going to celebrate. Don't you worry."

"How are we—"

I meld my lips to hers before she has the chance to finish her question. She gasps and I thrust my tongue into her mouth. Her taste of strawberries and sunshine hits me and I groan. I love her taste. I could get addicted to it. Hell, I'm halfway there already. I will never get enough.

She clings to my shoulders as I explore every inch of her mouth. I plan to thoroughly taste every single inch of her body today. I plan to—

We slam into the wall, and I tear my lips from hers.

"Bedroom. Now."

"Are you asking or telling?"

I raise an eyebrow. "Are you certain you want to tease me?"

"Why not? What are you going to do?"

I growl. "I'm going to tease that sass right out of you."

Her breath hitches. "You can try."

I press her against the wall. My hard length pushes into her stomach and her eyes flare. "I'll more than try. I'll have you begging me to stop teasing you. To sink my cock into your pussy."

She licks her lips. "Yes, please."

I smirk. "I do love it when you beg."

"I—"

I lift her and throw her over my shoulder.

"You better not drop me."

"I would never drop you. You're precious cargo."

I lay her on the bed and crawl on top of her. I love her being in this bed with me. She belongs here. But she's not here nearly enough. That shit changes tonight.

"I want to taste every single inch of you." She squirms beneath me. "Later. After I've had you for the first time."

Her eyes widen. "The first time?"

"Oh, sweetness, you have no idea." I kneel. "But first you need to be naked."

She reaches for the hem of her sweater but I bat her hands away. "You're mine to undress."

"I'm not yours."

"Hell, yes, you are," I grumble. "But I'm happy to show you you're mine over and over again."

She shivers. "O-o-o-kay."

I quickly undress her. I don't have time for slow today. Not if I'm going to fuck her more than once before Adele gets back home.

"And now the party can begin," I murmur once she's naked and laid out before me.

"Why aren't you naked?"

"Sweetness, if I'm naked, I'm inside you. And I need to prepare you first."

"Prepare away."

I smirk. "Thanks for your permission."

I press my lips to hers and she immediately opens for me. She may sass at me, but she doesn't deny me what we both want. What we both need. Her tongue reaches for mine and we duel until I growl to let her know playtime is over.

As I continue to explore her mouth, I draw my hand down her body. I stop at her breast to play for a while. I massage and knead the flesh until her nipple is a hard point. I pinch it and she moans before wrapping her legs around my waist.

She begins grinding against me and I unwind her legs from my hips. She mewls but I ignore the protest.

"Don't worry," I mutter against her lips. "I'll give you what you need."

"But you're too slow," she pouts.

"Do you want me to tease you instead?"

She groans.

I bite her lower lip. "Trust me." I soothe my tongue over her lip.

"I do trust you."

My heart contracts at her words. She trusts me. This woman, who wouldn't give me a chance because she was afraid I'd abandon her the way her dad did, trusts me.

I'm one step closer to getting her to fall in love with me. One step closer to ensuring she's latched onto me and won't let go.

I release her breast and trail my hand down her body until I reach her core. I bypass her clit and go straight for her pussy. I plunge a finger inside and moan at how hot and wet she is.

"You're dripping for me."

"What did you expect?" she asks in a breathy voice.

I add another finger and pump into her pussy until her walls tighten and quiver around me. I pause. I want those walls tightening and quivering around my cock. Not my fingers.

"Why did you stop?"

I remove my fingers and meet her gaze as I lick them clean. Her eyes flare and I can't resist tasting her mouth again.

"Do you taste how sweet you are?"

She moans in response and my cock weeps in my jeans. I need to be inside her. I need to feel her surrounding me. Her heat. Her scent. Her taste. I want it all.

I tear myself away from her lips and jump to my feet. I rip off my clothes before yanking open the bedside drawer and digging out a condom.

"I know you're on the pill, but I'll get tested before I go bare inside of you."

She nods. "Okay."

"No argument?"

"We're in a committed relationship, aren't we?"

She better not be questioning our relationship again. I growl. "Hell, yeah, we are, sweetness."

"It makes sense to ditch the condoms."

"I've never gone bare before."

"Never?"

"Never."

She smiles. "Good. I'll be your first."

And my last.

I climb back on the bed and fit myself between her legs. I notch my cock at her entrance.

"You're not leaving this bed."

Her brow wrinkles. "You can't keep me a prisoner in your bed."

I palm her cheek. "Not what I meant. You're not sneaking off to sleep in your bed after we fuck."

"I was planning on having dinner first."

"Sassy," I mutter. "Let me make myself perfectly clear. I want you sleeping in here beside me every night."

"But Adele…"

I squeeze her neck. "Adele is too young to know the difference." By the time she's old enough to understand, Sloane will have my ring on her finger.

"What about Boozer? He sleeps in bed with me."

"*I* sleep in bed with you. He'll sleep in his basket next to the bed."

She studies my face for a long moment before nodding. "Okay."

"Okay? You'll stay with me in this bedroom? No more bullshit about taking things slow?"

"It wasn't bullshit."

"Sloane," I growl.

"Yes. I'll stay with you since the word 'slow' doesn't seem to be part of your vocabulary."

I inch inside of her. "You think I can't do slow? Let me show you how slow I can be."

And I proceed to do just that.

Chapter 30

"Apparently, my dog and Zane's baby are in a love affair. Send help."

SLOANE

I wake when I hear Adele cry. Zane groans.

"I've got her."

"You don't have to," he protests through a yawn.

"You're tired. You worked hard last night."

He smirks. "Keeping you quiet when you come is a full-time job."

"Whatever," I mutter as I roll out of bed.

He captures my hand. "Seriously, sweetness, I can get her."

I kiss his cheek. "No need. I'm awake. Go back to sleep."

"Thank you."

"You don't have to thank me," I say but he's already asleep.

I pad out of the bedroom to the nursery. Adele is fussing in her crib. I pick her up.

"What's wrong, sweet baby? Are you hungry or do you need to be changed? Or both?" I sniff her diaper. "Definitely need a diaper change."

I quickly change her diaper and dress her for the day before preparing a bottle for her. I sit in the rocking chair in the corner of the nursery to feed her.

While she drinks from her bottle, I glance around the room. There are no longer boxes everywhere. Even Zane's office stuff is gone – relegated to the garage. It's a real nursery now.

The cupboard Jaxon put together is against one wall. It's filled with all the clothes that were in the other boxes and bags on the floor. On the opposite wall is the bookcase Eli assembled. There are some books, but there are also baskets filled with toys.

This is a room Adele can grow up in. I can't wait to experience it all. Her first tooth. The first time she walks. Her first day of school. I want to be there for it all.

Adele finishes her bottle. After I burp her, I rock her back to sleep. My heart is so full it could burst. I have everything I've ever wanted. A man I love. A baby I love. Adele isn't mine but I don't care. I love her.

Adele kicks out in her sleep. I sigh. I have to put her back in her crib.

Once she's settled, I aim for the kitchen. There's no sense trying to go back to sleep. I'm awake now. Coffee it is.

Coffee made. I grab my Kindle and return to the nursery to read in the rocking chair while Adele sleeps.

But when I check in the crib. Adele isn't alone. My dog is cuddled up to her.

"Boozer! Get out of there!"

He doesn't move – the little shit. I grab him by the collar and yank until he's forced to jump out of the crib.

"I can't believe you. Zane is going to kill me. And you're going to the glue factory."

Boozer whines and lies down in the middle of the room.

"You have to get out of here. I can't hide what you did if you stay here."

I pat his bottom and he sighs before heaving himself to his feet and trotting out of the room. Phew.

I clasp my chest as I wait for my heart rate to slow back down to normal.

Zane strolls into the room. Crap. Did he hear?

I force a smile. "I didn't expect you to wake this early."

He holds up the baby monitor. I drop my chin to my chest. I'm busted.

"Please don't kill me."

"You think I'm going to kill you because your dog jumped into the crib with Adele?"

There goes any hope he missed the entire episode.

"Yes?"

He barks out a laugh and I dare to lift my gaze to his. "I don't know what's funnier. How panicked you were when you found Boozer in the crib? Or how guilty you appeared when I walked in here?"

I narrow my eyes at him. "My guilty appearance isn't funny."

He throws his arms around me. "Wrong. It's hilarious. Don't ever play poker with my brothers. They'll clean us out of house and home."

I push him away. "I happen to be an excellent poker player."

"And you didn't look to the left just now either."

"Ugh!" I throw my hands in the air. "I haven't had enough coffee for you this morning."

He snags my coffee cup before threading his fingers through mine. "Let's get you some coffee, sweetness."

I practically melt. I love how he calls me sweetness. Not babe or darling or some other throwaway term. Zane makes me feel special in everything he does.

"Why don't I make you breakfast?" I offer.

His eyes widen. "You're going to make breakfast?"

I bristle. "I can make breakfast."

He raises an eyebrow. "And you didn't set off the smoke alarm toasting a bagel?"

"It was a Pop-Tart, not a bagel."

He chuckles. "Did the smoke alarm go off or not?"

I cross my arms over my chest. "Yes, but only because Adele had a blow-out and I forgot about the Pop-Tart."

"You're using our baby girl as an excuse."

No fair. He can't say our baby girl. It's cheating.

I glare. "Do you want breakfast or not?"

"What are you making? Burned bagels or burned Pop-Tarts?"

"I was going to make eggs and sausage, but I guess I can burn you a bagel."

"You can make eggs and sausage?"

I roll my eyes. "Who do you think made breakfast for Mom and all her boyfriends? It wasn't Mom."

He catches my hand and draws me onto his lap. "I'm sorry your mother didn't care for you the way she should have."

"It's okay. I'm over it."

"You're not, but you will be."

"What are you going to do? Snap your fingers and – voila! – I'm over it."

"Nope." He brushes my hair from my forehead. "I'm going to show you how real families act."

I want a real family. More than anything. But I'm afraid to reach for it.

Adele babbles over the baby monitor. "Baby girl is awake." Zane sets me on my feet. "We'll continue this conversation later."

He kisses me quick before strolling down the hallway toward the nursery. For someone who was scared of babies a year ago, he's a great dad.

Time to make some breakfast and show Zane I don't burn everything. I gather eggs and sausage from the refrigerator.

"Good morning, baby girl," Zane greets Adele over the baby monitor and I pause to listen to him as he begins to sing.

Rise and shine, baby mine. It's time to wiggle that cute behind. The sun's up high, the day's brand new, and Daddy's got a song for you.

I hear him making his way down the hallway and hustle to the stove to start on breakfast before he catches me eavesdropping.

"Here you go, baby girl." Zane lays her down on her playmat in the corner with her baby gym.

Boozer prances into the room and zeroes in on the baby. I wag my finger at him and he pauses. I return my attention to making breakfast.

Zane makes me a coffee and hands it to me with a kiss on my hair. "Smells good."

"I went with scrambled eggs since I didn't know what kind of eggs you prefer."

"Sounds good," he says before sitting at the table with his coffee and pulling out his phone.

I sigh. This morning is everything I've ever dreamed of. No one fighting. No one snarling at me. No one claiming I'm trying to steal her boyfriend.

Just a nice, peaceful, relaxing morning with the two people I love most in the world. I could get used to this. Fear tries to rear its ugly head but I shove it down. I refuse to ruin these moments because I'm afraid of the future.

I'll live in the moment. That's one good thing Mom tried to teach me. I never listened, though. It's hard to enjoy a good moment when you don't know if you're going to be homeless in the next one.

I shove thoughts of my childhood away and finish breakfast. As I'm bringing the plates to the table, I check on Adele.

I gasp. Boozer is laying next to her.

"Boozer," I growl.

Zane chuckles. "Your dog loves Adele."

"A little too much," I mutter.

I open the sliding door and motion to Boozer. "Come on. Go outside and do your business."

He barks before rushing outside. Adele cries and reaches for him.

Zane stands to pick her up. "It appears she loves Boozer as much as he loves her."

I grasp his hand to stop him. "Wait."

"What?"

I point to Adele. She's now on her front, trying to follow my dog. She grunts with frustration before pushing up and crawling.

I gasp. "She's crawling!"

Zane stares at her with his mouth gaping open. "My baby girl is crawling."

"Quick. We need to capture this moment. Where's your camera?"

When he doesn't move, I grab his phone from the table and begin snapping pictures. I probably take a dozen before Zane snaps out of it.

"I was in a group chat with my marketing masterclass." He frowns at the phone. "You've sent everyone the pictures of Adele."

"Oops. You can delete them."

"Oh, wait. Everyone is now sending pictures of what they're doing." He cringes. "I didn't need to see a man in a muscle shirt and white underwear this morning."

He drops his phone on the table and picks Adele up from the floor, where she's nearly made it to the door.

"Guess it's time to babyproof our home."

Our home. Those words slam into my chest before spreading warmth throughout my body. I have a home.

Chapter 31

"Nothing says 'team meeting' like Baby Shark and naked baby photos."

ZANE

I whistle as I send the email with the mock-up for our next marketing campaign. Once the other members of the board at *Buccaneer's Whiskey & Distillery* – also known as my brothers – approve the mock-up, the real work begins. I'm really proud of my ideas and excited to get started.

Rhett peeks into my office. "Oh, you're here. I was wondering who was whistling."

I frown at him. "I'm here. You can't complain about me missing work when Adele's sick. You do the same with Mira and Pearl."

He holds up a hand. "I'm not referring to when your kid is sick. I'm referring to you being here at all."

I scowl. "I work here. I'm the marketing manager or did you forget, old man?"

"Who do you think signs your paychecks?"

I roll my eyes. "No one uses paychecks anymore. Besides, Eli approves the payroll."

Eli is the CEO of the distillery, whereas Rhett is the CFO. Chief Financial Officer is the perfect position for Rhett. He's incredibly anal about numbers and enjoys guarding the finances.

While Eli worked two jobs so my brothers and I had money for extras growing up after my asshole dad left us, Rhett was the one protecting us – making sure we weren't bullied, checking we got our homework done, getting us to school on time.

Eli knocks on the door before strolling inside. "You ready for the meeting?"

"I don't have a meeting in my agenda. What meeting?"

"To discuss your email. You said you wanted to meet to discuss it."

"Have you even had a chance to read it?"

Miles skips into the room. "I haven't. I was too shocked to find out you were here."

I glare at him. He's the sales manager for the distillery. And he's in the office even less than me. His true love is surfing. He wanted to be a professional surfer until a rotator cuff injury in Hawaii stopped him. Nothing stops him from skipping the office for the waves now, though.

"I haven't traveled anywhere in ages."

"Oh right. Since you fell in love." Miles feigns throwing up.

"Don't be jealous of me because the woman you want won't give you the time of day."

He scowls. "I don't want Hazel."

Hazel was Miles's first girlfriend. They were together all through high school. But when he left for Hawaii – convinced his professional surfing career was about to explode – he dumped her. She's never forgiven him and I can't blame her.

Kai slaps Miles on the back as he joins us. "Someone's lying."

Miles elbows him. "I'm not lying."

"Liar. Liar. Surfboard on fire."

Miles flies at Kai but Rhett shoves his way between them. "Enough. This is an office."

"And we have a meeting," Jaxon adds as he arrives. He checks the time. "I'd appreciate more advance notice of a meeting in the future. I'm in the middle of taste testing a new batch of summer whiskey."

Miles perks up. "Taste testing?"

Kai rubs his hands together. "I'm in."

"Last one there's a rotten mermaid," Miles sings.

They start for the door but Jaxon blocks them. "I am not a stupid man."

Miles tries to push past him. "No one said you were."

Jaxon raises his eyebrow. "And yet you think I didn't lock my office where the samples are."

Kai chuckles. "As if a lock will stop us."

Jaxon smirks. "I added more security to my door after the last time you two hooligans rampaged it."

"Rampaged?" Kai clutches his chest. "I would never rampage a part of the distillery. I'm the operations manager."

"Being the operations manager didn't stop you from drinking all of my whiskey samples. And, once you were good and drunk, you decided to rearrange my office."

Kai bows to Jaxon. "You're welcome."

"It took me weeks to return everything to its proper place."

Miles places a hand over his heart. "I promise not to rearrange your office, no matter how much I'm tempted by your obsessive use of the alphabetical order."

A muscle in Jaxon's jaw ticks. "You will not be entering my office. End of discussion."

"But—"

Eli interrupts him. "There's whiskey in the conference room."

Miles's shoulders slump. "But it's not as fun as stealing Jaxon's samples."

Kai sighs. "Agreed."

Eli motions toward the hallway. "Shall we meet in the conference room to discuss Zane's proposal before he jets off somewhere on us?"

"Not fair. I haven't gone anywhere since Adele arrived."

"But now you officially have full custody," Eli says. "You can travel with her as much as you want."

I let the thought – Adele is mine! – warm me for a second before responding. "I'm not dragging my six-month-old baby around the world. We've barely managed to get her to sleep through the night."

"We, as in you and Sloane? How are things going?" Kai wiggles his eyebrows.

"I get why Miles wants to fight you."

"Thank you!" Miles lifts his hand and I slap it.

"If we're not having this meeting, I'm returning to my office," Jaxon declares.

"We're having the meeting." Eli herds everyone out of my office to the conference room.

Everyone takes their place except for Jaxon, who pulls on a pair of gloves to inspect his chair.

"What are you doing?" I ask.

"Ensuring someone didn't decide to coat the chair with molasses the way they did last time."

I chuckle. "You trying to get up was hilarious."

Miles grunts. "Easy for you to say. You didn't have to clean out the stills. I reeked for weeks."

Jaxon concludes his inspection and sits. "You shouldn't have pranked me."

Miles points to Kai. "He helped."

Kai raises his hands in the air. "I didn't help. You asked for molasses. I thought you were actually interested in the distilling process."

Rhett growls. "Can everyone please stop reminiscing about your past pranks? Some of us have families we want to get home to."

Eli and I nod in agreement.

Miles groans. "You might as well start a nursery here, as many babies as your partners keep on popping out."

"Technically." Eli holds up a finger. "My partner is the only one who 'popped out' a baby. But a nursery isn't a bad idea."

"I'm on it." Rhett flips open his notebook. "I'll make some calculations. Paying for a nanny is expensive."

"Not for everyone," Miles sings. "Raider brother number four, I'm looking at you."

I narrow my eyes at him. "Don't start with me."

He bats his eyelashes. "What? Is it not true? You don't pay Sloane, do you?"

I can't answer. I don't want him to know how Sloane was homeless when we began our arrangement. I won't embarrass her.

I grit my teeth. "Whatever happens between Sloane and me is none of your business."

He snorts. "It's totally my business when she cheats at I Spy."

I groan. "Not this again. You can't cheat at I Spy."

"She said the cloud resembled a grumpy monster. A cloud can't resemble a grumpy monster."

"Stop whining. You've cheated at plenty of games in your life."

Miles gasps. "I am not a cheater."

"This is why I stay in my lab," Jaxon mumbles. "These meetings are a waste of time."

Eli clears his throat. "Why don't you present your marketing idea, Zane?"

I stand and make my way to the front of the room. I log into the computer connected to the beamer and click on my presentation.

"Since we've decided to expand the distillery to include—"

I'm cut off when *Baby Shark* blares from the speakers. What the hell? This presentation isn't connected to music.

"I don't know, Zane. Sloane may enjoy pictures of you splashing in a bubble bath as a baby, but I don't think it'll sell many bottles of whiskey."

At Rhett's comment, I whirl around to look at the slideshow. Instead of my mock-ups for commercial ads for whiskey, there's a picture of me as a young child racing into the living room naked.

Eli stands and switches off the presentation. He slaps me on the back as he passes me. "Good to have you a part of the team, brother."

I scan his face for any signs of sarcasm, but he's being serious. I open my mouth to tell him I've always been a part of the team but I slam my mouth shut before I can utter the lie.

The truth is, I haven't always been a part of the team. I made sure to finish my work on time, but I wasn't here. I was gone as often as possible. Even if I was here, I didn't participate in the management of the company. Not in the way Eli envisioned when he founded the distillery to ensure all of the Raider brothers could stay on the island.

But things have changed. Since Adele arrived in my life, my priorities have changed. Canyoning in the Philippines doesn't hold the appeal it once did.

Now, I can't wait to go home and spend time with my baby and Sloane. Those two are what's important.

Chapter 32

"Small-town rule #1: kiss a Raider in public, and the island knows before you do."

SLOANE

I glance one last time in the mirror. No lipstick on my teeth? Check. No smudged mascara? Check. Jewelry, hair, shoes? Check. Check. Check. I'm ready.

Excitement buzzes through me as I exit my bedroom. Correction, my former bedroom. I'm now sleeping with Zane every night. But I dressed in here because I wanted to surprise him with a sexy outfit for our first big date.

"Whee-oo," Zane whistles when I reach the living room. He motions for me to twirl around and I do.

He catches my wrist and draws me near. "You're sexy, sweetness. But you can't ride my bike with a skirt on."

I push away from him. "Not a skirt." I kick one leg out. "It's a jumpsuit."

His gaze roves over my outfit.

"Are you studying how to get me out of this?"

He shrugs. "You can't blame me for being curious about what kind of bra you're wearing."

The jumpsuit has a deep v top. It's impossible to wear a bra with.

I bite my bottom lip and look up at him from beneath the lashes. "Maybe I'm not wearing a bra."

He groans. "You're killing me."

I smirk. "Goal achieved."

"Come on, sweetness. We need to leave now if we're going to make our reservation." He hands me a leather jacket. I don't complain how the jacket doesn't go with my outfit. I don't want to freeze on our way to the restaurant.

Once we're both dressed in leather jackets, he threads his fingers through mine and leads me outside. His motorcycle is already parked in the driveway.

"This is exciting! I've always wanted to ride on the back of a bike." I jump up and down. My breasts bounce with the movement but I'm too excited to care.

He moans. "Stop jumping. Riding a motorcycle with a hard-on is painful."

He adjusts himself in his jeans. My core tightens in response. Not wearing a bra was definitely the right choice.

"Maybe we should skip dinner." My voice comes out all breathy since I'm imagining all the ways we could spend our time if we don't go out.

"Not a chance. I want to take you out. Show you a good time. We haven't been out without Adele. I love my baby girl, but you're important, too."

Warmth spreads through me. "For someone who doesn't do relationships, you're really good at saying the right thing."

He snags a helmet from the handlebars and places it on my head. "Only for you, sweetness."

"Stop being perfect. I want my ride on a motorcycle."

He smirks. "You think I'm perfect."

Yes, I do. But Zane Raider has a big enough ego as it is. I'm not inflating it.

I try to tie the helmet strap but he bats my hands away. "I've got it."

He secures the strap before kissing my nose. He puts on his helmet and straddles the bike. It's a good thing I wore panties tonight because they're wet after that sexy move.

"Put your foot…"

I wave away his directions. I haven't been on the back of a bike before but I know how to get on one. I've watched my mother hop on a bike and ride off into the sunset enough times.

Once I'm settled, Zane takes my hands and wraps them around his waist. "Hold on tight."

He doesn't need to tell me twice. I'm holding onto him as tight as I can. For as long as I can.

He switches on the motor and I can feel the vibrations coursing through my body. I'm enjoying this ride already, and we haven't even left the driveway.

"Ready?"

I squeeze his waist. "Ready."

I expect him to shoot out of the driveway and down the road. I've seen him do it enough times in the past. But he gently drives to the end of the driveway before slowly driving down the street.

"Faster!"

He nods, but he doesn't increase our speed.

"Zane, faster."

He goes a tiny bit faster. We can now pass people walking but not any runners. This is ridiculous.

"I want to go faster." It's a good thing these helmets are linked up with microphones. Otherwise, I would have lost my voice already from yelling at him to speed the hell up.

"I don't want to hit Sammy."

"Sammy isn't out and about in January and you know it. It's entirely too cold for him to be up to his old tricks."

Sammy is a seal that decided to make Smuggler's Hideaway his home. He enjoys sunbathing in the middle of the road and planting himself in front of people's doors so they can't get out of their houses.

"I'm being careful. I have precious cargo on my bike today."

I sigh. How can I complain about how slow we're going now?

"This precious cargo wants to drive faster than a golf cart."

He waits until we've left the town limits of Smuggler's Rest to speed up. It's enough to feel the wind whip along my body.

"Whoo-hoo!"

He chuckles. "You enjoy being on the back of my bike."

I squeeze him. "I enjoy being wrapped around you."

"This is going to be the longest dinner ever."

"My offer to skip dinner and spend the evening in bed still stands."

"You're going to pay for teasing me later, sweetness."

My nipples pebble in response to the promise in his voice. "Yes, please."

We arrive at *Hideaway Haven Resort* and Zane parks in a spot near the front. He helps me off before pushing down the kickstand and switching off the motor. Sexy. But not as sexy as him mounting the bike.

I remove my helmet and bend over to fluff out my hair. "Is it bad?"

Zane clasps my hand and pulls. I slam into his body. "Is it bad you look like I just fucked you in the backseat of my car?"

"We didn't drive a car," I breathe out.

He growls before his lips are on mine. I don't hesitate to open for him. I know how good his tongue feels exploring my mouth. And how good he tastes. I wrap my arms around his shoulders and hold on for the ride.

"Sloane!"

Zane tears his lips from mine. "To be continued," he murmurs.

"Nova," I greet the woman.

Her gaze ping-pongs between me and Zane. "The rumors are true."

"I thought you didn't listen to rumors ever since high school."

She growls. "Those cheerleaders were big fat liars."

I giggle. Nova had the biggest crush on Hudson, the football quarterback, back in high school. The cheerleaders used to make up stories about how they were dating Hudson, who was clueless about the whole situation.

Nova won in the end, though. Since she's now married to Hudson – who was an NFL player until he got injured – and they have a little baby girl, Iliana.

"Doesn't change the message. You shouldn't listen to rumors."

"I don't need to listen to rumors when I caught you and Zane Raider making out next to his motorcycle in front of my husband's resort."

I feel my cheeks heat. When Zane touches me, I forget where I am.

Zane throws an arm around my shoulders. "You can't blame me. She's irresistible in this outfit."

Nova's gaze rakes over me. "I get what you're saying."

The warmth on my cheeks is blistering now. I clear my throat. "We should get going. We have a reservation."

"Have fun."

As we stroll toward the entrance, I can see Nova out of the corner of my eye digging out her phone. I groan. "The entire island will hear about us kissing within two minutes."

Zane scowls and stutters to a halt. "Do you care? Are you embarrassed to be with me?"

My jaw drops open and I stare up at his deep blue eyes I want to drown in. "You can't be serious."

"I'm dead fucking serious."

"Have you—"

"Excuse me," someone says as they scoot around us.

Shit. We're standing in the doorway to an exclusive resort having this conversation.

"Can we go somewhere private to discuss this?"

"No," Zane grumbles. "If you're embarrassed of being with me, I want to know right the fuck now."

"You have lost your mind."

He spins on his heel and heads toward his motorcycle.

"I'm not embarrassed of you!" I shout after him and he stops. He doesn't turn around, but I know he's listening. "But I'm not my mom. I don't cause drama by having arguments with my partner in front of the entire world."

Except everyone in the foyer of the resort is now frozen while listening to me shout at Zane. So much for not becoming my mom.

Zane marches to me and sweeps me into his arms. "Fuck, sweetness. I'm sorry. I shouldn't have pushed you. I was worried you were embarrassed of me because I used to be a player."

I bury my face in his shoulder and snuggle into his embrace. "You're not who you used to be, and I'm not who I used to be either."

He pinches my chin and lifts my face. "I'm fucking proud of you. And proud to be the man with you."

I love you.

I manage to keep those three precious words inside. I'm not confessing my love while we're standing in the doorway of an exclusive hotel where no one bothers to hide how they're eavesdropping on our conversation.

"I'm proud of you and proud to be with you, too."

He smiles down at me and his dimples make an appearance. I want our children to have those dimples. I bite my tongue before I tell him as much.

"You wanna skip dinner and go for a ride?"

"Yes."

I barely have a chance to respond before he starts dragging me to his bike.

"But you better feed me at some point."

"Oh, I'll feed you. Don't you worry."

I have a feeling he's not referring to food. My body shivers in response.

How did I get this lucky? Zane is not only sexy and can use his body to bring me more joy than I've ever experienced before. But he's also sweet and kind and considerate.

Falling in love with him was inevitable.

Chapter 33

"Thought Adele was the handful today. Turns out, nope."

ZANE

I groan when Adele reaches the television cabinet. She manages to open the drawer and begins pulling out remote controls.

I rush to her. "No, baby girl."

Sloane enters the living room with our coffees and scans the mound of remotes on the ground. "I was gone two minutes."

"She started crawling a few days ago. I didn't realize she'd be the Olympic champion of crawling within days."

Sloane snorts. "She's your daughter. What did you expect? I'm surprised she's not skateboarding yet."

I lift Adele into the air and blow bubbles onto her stomach. "Who's my little skateboarder?" She giggles. "Shall we take her to the park today?"

"Um, dude, I think she's a bit young for the skateboard park."

"I don't know. I bet she could sit on a skateboard while I push her around."

"Remind me to buy her a baby helmet."

"You can buy her a baby helmet later. Let's go to the park."

It's Saturday and I'm off all day. Sloane has to work later tonight but she can spend the majority of the day with us. I'm hoping once she's officially appointed assistant manager, she'll work fewer evenings. I miss going to bed with her.

Between waking up at two in the morning to fuck her and middle of the night feedings for Adele, my sleep pattern is completely out of whack.

Miles found me asleep on the toilet at work the other day. I don't know who was more surprised. Him, when he barged in on me, or me when I woke up and forgot I was sitting on a toilet with my pants around my ankles?

"As long as we stick to the baby swings."

I bat my eyelashes. "What about the slide?"

"Fine. But you're helping her down. The last time I was on the slide, some kid's diaper blew up in front of me."

I chuckle. "It's a good thing I've mastered getting shit stains out of laundry."

"Words I never thought I'd hear Zane Raider say in this lifetime."

Does she realize I'm a changed man? That I don't want to chase other women? That she's the only woman I see?

"I'll change her while you get the diaper bag."

Sloane raises her eyebrow. "You're volunteering to change her diaper?"

"I change her diaper."

She snorts. "When there's no choice in the matter."

"Whatever," I mutter since she's not wrong.

I do try and avoid changing her diaper. But who can blame me? The smells that come out of this little baby girl are rancid.

And this is from someone who once fell into a sewer. Parkouring is not for the faint of heart. Especially when you're in a country with open sewers. I don't recommend parkour in Nigeria.

"Do you have a dirty diaper?" I ask Adele as I carry her to the nursery. I set her down on the changing table and tickle her tummy. She giggles. "Who's my beautiful girl?"

The doorbell rings.

"I'll get it." Sloane points to Adele. "You get her diaper changed."

"If it's my brothers, tell them to fudge off."

I cringe at the word fudge. But I can't afford to swear anymore. Not since Sloane started a swear jar. She says Adele is old enough to imitate sounds and we need to be cautious. She doesn't want Adele entering kindergarten 'swearing like a sailor on shore leave'.

By the time I finish changing Adele's diaper and dressing her, Sloane hasn't returned. Crap. My brothers are here. So much for a quiet Saturday morning at the park with Adele and Sloane.

But when I enter the living room, I'm not greeted by Raiders. It's Sloane's mom instead. I'd prefer my brothers – pranks included.

"Poppy." I nod in greeting.

"Zane." She licks her lips and my stomach sours. Sloane deserves to have a mother who doesn't come on to her boyfriend. "I have fabulous news."

Sloane groans. "I'm not sponsoring your journey into space."

Poppy scowls. "It was deep sea, not space."

Crap. Poppy is an adventurer? No wonder Sloane kept her distance from me. It was bad enough, I was a player, but I must have reminded her of her mother. She probably thinks I'm the same as her mother. I'm not. I don't shirk my responsibilities.

"What do you want?" Sloane asks.

"It's not what I want. It's what I have."

Sloane's nose wrinkles and retreats a step. "If you came here with a communicable disease, I'm kicking you out."

"Must you always cause drama. I don't have any disease."

"Okay. Fine. I'll bite. What do you have?"

Poppy reaches into her bag and flourishes an envelope. "Tickets to Japan! I know you've always wanted to visit."

If Sloane wants to visit Japan, I'll take her. But maybe she wants to go with her mom. My chest tightens, and breathing becomes impossible. Is this the moment Sloane abandons me? Will she disappear with her mom?

I study her. She's not jumping for joy or rushing off to pack her bags. She's irate. Her nostrils flare while her hands fist at her waist. I blow out a breath in relief.

"You think," she says between clenched teeth, "you can waltz in here with tickets and I'll run away with you?"

"It's what you've always wanted."

"Always wanted?" Sloane rears back. "What I wanted was a mother who paid attention to me. Who cared for me. Who protected me when her boyfriends leered at me."

I growl. Her mother's boyfriends leered at her? If they touched her, I won't give a shit how Poppy is Sloane's mother. She's done.

Poppy flicks her hair over her shoulder. "No one ever touched you."

Sloane pounds a fist on her chest. "I didn't feel comfortable in my home."

"You always were such a sensitive little thing."

"I'm sensitive because I wanted to feel safe in my home? Because I didn't want my mother's boyfriends to chase after me? Because I didn't want to lock my bedroom door at night?"

Poppy sighs. "The past is the past. There's nothing we can do to change it now."

Sloane starts for her mom but I shackle her wrist to stop her. "Don't do anything you'll regret."

"Trust me. I won't regret it."

"Yes, you will. You have a kind heart, sweetness. Hurting your mother will destroy you."

She sags. "Fine."

I release her wrist and wrap my arm around her shoulders. I'm presenting a united front to her mother. Her mother didn't protect her. But I will.

"I don't know why I bothered coming here," Poppy mutters.

"Why don't you visit Japan with your boyfriend?" Sloane asks.

Poppy's lips purse. "I'm currently in between boyfriends."

Sloane lifts a brow. "By choice?"

"It was a silly misunderstanding."

"A silly misunderstanding that resulted in you having enough money to buy plane tickets to Japan?"

"I didn't know the ring was a family heirloom. I wouldn't have pawned it had I known."

Sloane stares at her mother with disgust. "Right. It was an accident."

Poppy perks up. "I'm glad you understand. Now, let's go visit Japan as a family. The flight departs in a few hours. Plenty of time to pack."

"As a family?" I growl.

She blinks at me. "Yes, a family. I'm her mother."

"You're not her mother. You're the egg donor."

"I did more than donate my egg. I carried her for nine months. The things I had to do to get my body back in shape. And I raised her."

"You didn't raise her. You didn't love and cherish her. You didn't teach her about morals and ethics. You didn't show her how to be a good person."

I turn to Sloane. "You're an amazing person. You could have gone off the rails, but you didn't."

"Technically, I tried. But the inhabitants of Smuggler's Hideaway weren't having it. The mayor, Lana, stopped by when I was visiting a jail cell and gave me a dressing down. I've never been so ashamed in my life."

"Visiting a jail cell?"

"For one night only."

I chuckle. "What did you do?"

"It was a misunderstanding."

I raise an eyebrow.

"Fine," she huffs. "I accidentally spray painted Kira's garage door."

"How do you accidentally spray paint?"

"Easy, really. You accidentally buy the paint and then accidentally find yourself at someone's house in the middle of the night. It could happen to anyone."

"I…" I cut myself off before I tell her I love her. It's too early for proclamations of love. And I'm not telling her how I feel in front of her mother.

"Hello!" Speaking of her mother. "Did you forget I was here? Go pack your things. We don't have all day."

"I'm not going with you."

Poppy stomps her foot. "But I'm your family."

"Wrong. Zane and Adele are my family."

Relief courses through me with such fervor I nearly drop Adele. Sloane isn't going anywhere. She's staying right here where she belongs. Thank fuck.

I kiss her cheek before handing her the baby. "I'll escort your mother out."

"Well, I never!" Poppy shouts.

I herd her toward the door. I don't touch her. I wouldn't put it past her to call the police on me. But I do get her to the door.

She glances back at her daughter, who shoos her away. Good. She's not mad at me for kicking her mom out of our home.

Poppy steps onto the porch and I shut the door on her.

This isn't the end of Sloane's problems with Poppy. She'll be back again. And I'll be here ready to pick up the pieces of Sloane's heart every time. Because I'm someone she can rely on. Forever.

Chapter 34

"Reminder: hospitals are not good places for impromptu games of hide-and-seek."

SLOANE

I rock Adele but she doesn't stop crying. "Come on, sweetie pie. You need to calm down."

Adele does not agree with me. I rub her back, but it has no effect.

I stand and pace around the room. "Do you want me to sing to you? Daddy's the singer. Not me. But I'll give it a try."

I hum, but every lyric I've ever known escapes my mind.

I dig my phone out of my pocket and open my music app. I nearly fumble the phone when AC/DC blares. Adele wails even louder. I close the app and throw my phone on the changing table.

"I don't blame you, sweetie pie."

I bounce her as I meander around the house. Usually, she'll calm down when she's moving. Maybe I should put her in her stroller and go for a walk. Good idea. We'll go for a walk.

But when I set her in her stroller, I notice her face is flushed and her neck is stiff. Oh no. Oh no, oh no, oh no.

I place my hand on her forehead. She's burning up.

I don't hesitate. I dig my... Crap. Where is my phone?

"Stay here, sweetie pie." I rush to the nursery and snatch my phone from the changing table.

I dial Jessica as I hurry back to Adele.

"He—"

"Adele's sick. What do I do?"

"Sick how? Is she throwing up?"

"I think she has a fever. Her face is flushed."

"Did you take her temperature?"

"Her neck is stiff, and I haven't changed her diaper in hours."

"I'll meet you at the hospital."

I hang up without saying goodbye and bundle Adele into her coat before racing outside to the dad-mobile. Lucky for me, Zane keeps the car here when Adele is home.

"Call Zane," I shout once the Bluetooth is connected.

"Hey, sweetness. What's up?"

"Adele. Sick. Hospital."

"Slow down. What's happening?"

"Adele has a fever. I'm on my way to the hospital."

"I'll meet you there."

I drive to the hospital and park the car in front of the emergency room. Zane is waiting for me with his mom in front of the doors.

He wrenches the rear door open and picks up Adele. I follow him inside.

Jessica trails after us. "I spoke to Dr. Allens. She has a room for us."

Zane marches to the room where the doctor is waiting for us. "This must be baby Adele." She motions to the bed. "Lay her down. I'll examine her."

A nurse rushes into the room. "Let's give the doctor room to work."

She tries to herd us outside but Zane doesn't move. "I'm not leaving my baby."

"You must be mommy?" she says to me.

Before I have a chance to answer, Zane does. "She's not the baby's mom. She's the nanny."

Pain lances through me. Is that what Zane thinks? I'm merely the nanny? He didn't say I'm his girlfriend or his partner. He said nanny. Someone who isn't a member of the family.

"I'll… ah…" I motion toward the door but no one's paying any attention to me.

I back out of the room. But once I'm in the hallway, I don't know where to go or what to do. Should I stay? I don't feel welcome here. But Adele is sick. I don't want to abandon her.

She's the nanny.

Zane's words echo in my mind. No matter how much I want to stay, I'm not welcome here. Zane doesn't need me.

Maybe I should go home. Home. I've been searching for a home my entire life. I thought I finally found one. But maybe I was wrong. I'm not Zane's girlfriend or his partner. *She's the nanny.*

I head for the exit. Shit. Zane's car is still parked in front of the entrance to the ER, blocking everyone. I quickly move the car and give the keys to the nurse at the desk.

I wring my hands as I stand in front of the exit, trying to decide what to do. I don't want to leave until I know Adele is going to be okay. But I'm the nanny. I'm not welcome here.

I notice Jaxon, Kai, Miles, and Eli piling out of Rhett's truck. My decision is made. I'm not staying here with the Raider family. I thought I was one of them. I thought I found a family.

She's the nanny.

I'm such an idiot. I thought Zane had changed his ways. I should have known better. People don't change. Look at my mother.

Miles waves as he approaches me. Escape! I need to escape!

I race toward the front entrance but Stuart is coming in that way. I spin around. There must be another exit.

There! An employee only hallway. I'll hide there until the Raiders are all gathered together in the waiting room and then sneak out the front.

I peek through the window of the door to make sure there's no one in the hallway before pushing it open.

"We're still waiting on the lab results."

"The lab should have had those results by now."

Oh no! Someone's coming. More than someone, by the sounds of it. I scan the area.

Storage closet. Perfect. I rush to it. It's unlocked. Finally. Something's going right for me. I enter and shut the door behind me.

I don't dare switch on the light. Instead, I stand perfectly still in the middle of the closet and wait for the people to pass me.

Shoes squeak on the tile floor as they pass. I blow out a breath. Phew. That was a close call.

I reach for the doorknob but the door opens and the light switches on.

"Ah!"

"Ah!"

We both scream in surprise.

The nurse grasps her chest. "What are you doing in here? I told Robert he wasn't allowed to play hide and seek anymore."

Robert? Who's Robert? Wait a sec. I don't care. I go with it.

I shrug. "You know Robert."

"Go on." She motions me into the hallway. "Get out of here before Dr. Stick in the Mud sees you."

She doesn't have to tell me twice. I rush down the hallway and out the front door. But when I start for my vehicle, I realize I don't have one. I'm stranded.

"Thanks for picking me up," I say when I climb into Parker's car ten minutes later.

"Not a problem."

Parker and I have been friends since I arrived on the island. Unfortunately, we don't have a chance to meet up often since she works crazy hours operating her bakery.

"How's Jeremy?"

Another reason we haven't had much chance to meet up. She fell in love with a billionaire who was visiting the island for Christmas. Lucky girl.

"I'll tell you all about him if you tell me why I had to pick you up from the hospital when you obviously aren't injured."

I sigh. "What are the chances you don't already know?"

She shrugs. "I know Adele is sick since Jeremy was having a meeting with Eli when Eli found out."

I forgot her boyfriend and Eli are partners. They founded *Apparoo,* a multi-billion-dollar company that develops apps for your phone.

"What I don't know is why the little baby girl you love is sick in the hospital and yet you're calling me for a ride."

I study the passing scenery as tears well in my eyes. "It's a long story," I manage to say before the damn breaks and tears pour down my face.

She pats my arm. "I'm sorry. I didn't intend to make you cry."

"You didn't." I sniff. "Zane Asshole Raider did."

"Asshole? Strange middle name."

"Don't be funny. It's not funny. Nothing's funny. Nothing will ever be funny again."

I sob and she stops on the side of the road to pull me into her arms. It's awkward since we're in the front seat of the car, but I cling to her anyway. I'll accept whatever comfort I can get.

She rubs her hand up and down my back until I've exhausted all the tears I have. I'm sure I'll cry more later, but for now, my tear ducts have dried up. I pull away and lean against the passenger seat.

"Where am I driving you?"

I groan. I have nowhere to go. This is what I get for dating my boss. Have I mentioned lately what an idiot I am?

"I have an idea." She puts the car into gear and drives toward Smuggler's Rest.

"I'm not staying with you and Jeremy. No offense, but all your lovey-dovey stuff will turn me into a homicidal maniac."

"Turn you into a maniac? You're not already one?"

"Not a homicidal one."

"Good point. But you're not staying with me and Jeremy. I have the perfect place for you."

"I'm not committing a crime, so I can spend the night in jail. I don't care how nice the jail cells are since Eli invested in them."

She giggles. "The mayor will tan your hide if she finds out you're in jail again."

"Technically, I promised I wouldn't spend another night in jail for a decade. It's been more than a decade."

"You sound like a Raider."

I gasp.

"Shit. I didn't mean to bring him up. Pretend I didn't say anything."

I slump in my seat. "Work tomorrow is going to be fun. The whole town will know by then."

"By then? The whole town knows now."

I growl. "You're not helping things."

"I'm being realistic."

Ugh. Why did I beg my mom to stay in Smuggler's Hideaway when I was twelve? I should have let her follow her boyfriend to Belize. I could have learned Spanish.

Anything would be better than living in a town where everyone pities me because the man I love thinks of me as his nanny.

Chapter 35

"I can add idiot to the list of skills on my resume."

ZANE

I cuddle Adele into my arms. I allow her sweet baby scent to wash away the fear. I can't lose her. She's my pride and joy. I never expected her. I thought I didn't want children. But since she arrived, everything has changed.

"I'll have the nurse draw up the discharge papers," Dr. Allens says.

"Thanks, doc. I'm sorry we panicked."

She grins. "You were right to come to the hospital. She only has the flu, but with her symptoms, it's better to be safe than sorry."

Mom squeezes my shoulder. "It's okay, Zane. She's perfectly fine."

"How did you do this?"

"Do what?"

"Raise six boys who were in and out of the hospital our entire youth without having a heart attack."

"You take it day by day. Sometimes hour by hour."

"Thank you."

"There's no need to thank me. I'll always come running when one of my boys or my grandchildren needs me."

"No." I shake my head. "Not thank you for coming today. Although, I appreciate it. I mean, thank you for all you did for us while we were growing up. You were the best mom. I don't think I ever told you."

She kisses my cheek. "You never need to thank me for being your mom. It was and is my privilege."

"I was so busy being mad at Dad for abandoning us and trying not to become him, I forgot I had a support system."

"It didn't stop you from giving Stuart a hard time when we began dating."

I smirk. "It's my duty as your son to give any man you date a hard time."

"Maybe, but I could have done without you setting his house on fire."

I roll my eyes. "We didn't set his house on fire. It was merely a bit of smoke. And it was an accident."

She laughs. "I hope your children are as rambunctious as you are."

"Adele is the perfect baby girl. There's no way she's ever going to sprint naked through downtown while being chased by sheep."

She pats my back. "You keep on thinking that."

"But my next child?" I shrug. "Who knows?" I scan the room. "Speaking of which, where's Sloane?"

Mom blinks. "I don't know."

She's obviously lying. Mom never loses sight of anyone in her pack. "Mom?"

"Let's get those discharge papers. Your brothers are waiting to hear how Adele is doing."

I should have realized the Raider clan is here. We always show up for one another. Except for when I'm off on an adventure. I glance down at Adele. She's the only adventure I need now.

We're swarmed by my brothers the second we reach the waiting room. Adele is handed around until I growl and declare no more.

"Where's Sloane?" I ask as I scan the room.

"We should go." Eli herds us out of the hospital into the parking lot.

"What about Sloane? She needs a ride," I say as I strap Adele into the car seat.

Miles jumps into the driver's seat. "I've always wanted to drive the dad-mobile."

He switches on the car and drives out of the parking lot. "Wait. What about Sloane?"

"Did you switch off your computer before you left the distillery?" Kai asks.

"I don't know. I wasn't exactly thinking about computer protocol."

We arrive at home. "Thanks for the ride," I say as I release Adele from the child seat. She doesn't wake up. The doctor said she'll sleep a lot for the next day or two.

I assume my brothers will return to work at the distillery now but they follow me into the house. "I need to get Adele settled."

I place my baby girl in her crib and grab the baby monitor. I search my bedroom and the spare bedroom, but Sloane isn't here. Did we leave her at the hospital?

"What's going on?" I ask when I enter the living room, where my brothers are waiting for me. "Every time I brought up Sloane's name, you changed the subject. And she's not here."

"We wanted you to get Adele settled before bringing up the topic," Eli says.

"The topic? Sloane isn't a topic. She's my girlfriend."

He lifts a brow. "She is?"

"What the hell? Of course, she is. She lives here with me and Adele."

"But you didn't refer to her as your girlfriend, did you?" Rhett asks.

"What are you talking about? Why is everyone being mysterious? If you're about to pull a prank after I spent the afternoon in the hospital with my daughter, I'm going to lose my mind."

Rhett holds up his hands. "This isn't a prank."

I meet Jaxon's gaze. He's the only one I can trust to tell the truth. "It's not a prank."

"Okay. If this isn't a prank, why all the mystery? Is Sloane okay? Is she hurt?"

"Depends on how you define hurt," Kai mumbles.

"What are you talking about?" I rub a hand over my forehead. "You're giving me a headache."

Eli motions to the couch. "Maybe you should sit down."

"Maybe you should tell me what the hell is going on before I forget I have a baby sleeping in the other room and punch you."

He frowns. "Sloane isn't here."

"Obviously. Where is she?"

He shrugs. "We're actually not certain."

I gasp. "You're not certain? What happened? And why didn't anyone tell me?"

"Don't panic," Rhett says.

Too late. I'm imagining all the horrible things that could have happened to Sloane. Was she kidnapped? Did she have an accident? Where is she?

"Sloane is with Parker," he continues.

Relief knocks into me with such force I nearly stumble. I lock my limbs before I fall on my ass.

"Why didn't you say so to begin with? It's weird she's visiting a friend when Adele is sick, but maybe Parker needed her."

Sloane doesn't have many friends but she's loyal to those she has. She wouldn't hesitate to rush to Parker's side if her friend needed help.

"Parker didn't need her. Sloane ran away," Kai says.

My brow wrinkles. "Ran away?" Why would she run away? What am I missing here?

"She freaked out when you referred to her as the nanny."

"What? Sloane isn't the nanny. She's my girlfriend."

"Except you called her your nanny at the hospital."

"I didn't…" I trail off when I realize I did call her the nanny. "I was only making sure the doctor knew Sloane isn't Adele's biological mother in case it was important for whatever was wrong with the baby."

Kai grimaces. "Sloane obviously didn't realize that."

"Hold on. Are you saying Sloane ran away because I called her the nanny?"

He nods.

I growl. "I fucking love her and she bails the second I make one mistake?"

"Dude." Miles shakes his head.

I glare at him. "Don't you dude me. I'm not the one who dumped the woman I love because I wouldn't have time for her after I got famous."

He flinches. "Yeah, I screwed up big time. Which is why I know how much you screwed up."

"It was one mistake. I was worried about my baby girl."

Rhett points to a chair. "Sit."

"I—"

"Sit." I plonk down on the sofa. I cross my arms over my chest to indicate how unhappy I am with my older brother ordering me around. I'm not a child.

"Actually." Jaxon clears his throat. "I should handle this one."

Rhett motions for him to proceed.

"I almost lost the love of my life because I said something stupid." Jaxon fiddles with his glasses. "I was being an idiot because I was afraid Blossom was going to leave me. It was a preemptive strike."

"It was stupid," Kai mutters.

Jaxon nods. "It was stupid. But insecurities run deep. Dad abandoning us fucked with my head. I can't imagine how it feels to have never met your father. And then your mother, instead of working her ass off to show you you're loved, chases after other men and leaves you on your own. Sloane never had a home, Zane."

"I know. I was trying to give her one."

"But when the nurse asked if she was the mother, you said she was your nanny. Imagine how she felt. The man she loves, the father to the little baby girl she loves, thinks of her as the nanny."

"I don't think of her as the nanny."

Jaxon raises his brow. "You don't?"

"Of course not. I love her."

"Have you ever told her you love her?" Eli asks.

"No. I was planning this big event to tell her. A night at the resort with rose petals and all of that romance shit."

Rhett squeezes my shoulder. "She doesn't know how you feel."

"How can she not know? I show her I love her every day."

Rhett sighs. "Sloane has never known love. She doesn't understand what you were doing."

I open my mouth to argue with him. How can Sloane not know I love her? I moved her into my bedroom. I made her part of our little family.

Our little family. A nanny isn't part of the family.

"Shit." I bury my face in my hands. "What am I going to do?"

Chapter 36

SLOANE

Boozer nudges my shoulder with his cold, wet snout. I push him away.

"Not now, Boozer boy. I'm trying to sleep."

He barks and I force my eyes open to make certain there's not a reason he's ignoring my need for sleep. I startle at the vision in front of me.

I'm not in Zane's bedroom in his home. No adorable baby girl is sleeping in the nursery across the hall. No sexy man is laying next to me with his arm wrapped around my waist. Because I'm in the loft above Parker's bakery.

Don't get me wrong. The loft is adorable. It's a big, airy room with gorgeous exposed wooden beams overhead. The kitchen gleams with copper accents and sea-glass cabinet knobs. The bed, while not in a separate bedroom, is hidden in a nook.

And there's no one to complain about Boozer's barking. Except for this loft above *Pirate's Pastries,* the main drag in downtown doesn't have any housing. It's all shops and restaurants.

It's the perfect place for me to live with my overenthusiastic dog. My stomach sours. I was living in the perfect place.

Until Zane crapped all over my dream. I thought he'd changed his ways. I thought he cared for me. I thought—

Who cares what I thought? I was obviously wrong.

I roll out of bed and Boozer dances around – excited it's time for a walk.

I check the time. Shit. It's going to be a short walk straight to his doggy walker since I need to be at work in less than an hour.

Apparently, I sleep all day when I'm heartbroken. Not sure what I can do with the information since I don't plan to ever risk my heart again. I never should have risked my heart with Zane to begin with.

But I couldn't resist him. He's always been a sexy man – those ocean blue eyes, that square jaw, those wide shoulders – but when he cradled Adele in his arms? I got weak and forgot about all the reasons I avoided him in the past.

My chest burns. I rub a hand over it, but it doesn't calm the burn. Nothing seems to. Not copious amounts of beer. Not mounds of food. Not hours of crying. Not even spending time with Parker, who's a saint for putting up with me and my whining. She even gave me this loft for a bargain basement rental price.

Enough wallowing in my pain. I've never been much of a wallower. Although, I've never let anyone hurt me the way Zane did before.

Stop it, Sloane!

He never promised me a rose garden. He never said he loves me. This is on me. I jumped in with both feet and didn't bother bringing a raincoat for those less than sunny days.

I never should have dated the man I was living with and working for. Speaking of work. I need to get going before I'm late for my job at *Rumrunner.*

"You're here," Harper says when I enter the bar forty-five minutes later.

I check the time. "I'm not late. I'm five minutes early."

"I just thought…." She trails off and clears her throat. "Never mind."

"You thought I'd blow up my entire life because your brother-in-law broke my heart."

"He's not my brother-in-law yet."

I roll my eyes. As if Zane's status in her life is the important part of what I said.

"But, yeah, I thought you might need some time off."

"I'm good."

I'm not. But I will be. After all, no one has more experience with being disappointed by the people she loves than me. Good ole Mom taught me all about disappointment. And getting back up afterwards.

"You're stronger than I ever gave you credit for."

I flex my biceps, which are frankly nothing to write home about. "Unstoppable."

She giggles. "As long as you don't break out in song."

"Don't worry. I'm well aware of how tone deaf I am."

"Boss," Dave hollers and we both turn to him. Oops. Harper is the big boss here. Obviously.

"Sorry." I back away. "This is on you."

"Actually." Dave points at me. "You're the one I need."

"I'll be there in two minutes."

"No rush."

But I do rush. I want to be a person the employees of this bar can count on. I'm not the flighty woman who is never on time. Not anymore.

I hang my coat up in the storage area and tie a server apron around my waist. I don't bother checking my hair or make-up. I look like shit and I know it.

I make my way behind the bar. "What do you need, Dave?"

"Not me. Him." He points across the room to where Zane is standing, holding Adele with all of his brothers surrounding him.

I knew I'd have to deal with the Raider brothers at some point. They do love this bar. Especially since Kai and Harper are in love and engaged to be married. But I thought I'd at least have a few days to get used to the idea.

I guess not.

Zane catches my eye and strolls to the bar. I want to jump over the bar and run to him. To beg him to give me another chance to prove to him, I can be more than a nanny. I can be anything he needs or wants.

I push those thoughts away. I know better. Zane is a player who loves adventures. He's never settling down.

I scowl at him. "Zane. We've discussed this. You shouldn't bring a baby to the bar."

"Not even when her mother is here?"

I scan the room. "Daisy's here? What a bitch. I'm going to enjoy kicking her out."

I march out from behind the bar, intent on finding Daisy and dealing with her, but Zane shackles my wrist to stop me.

"Daisy isn't here."

"But you said Adele's mother is here."

"She is. I'm looking right at her."

His gaze meets mine.

"I'm confused."

"You, sweetness, are her mother. More than her birth mother ever has been."

I must be hallucinating. Zane isn't saying what I think he is. He's probably telling me he packed up all my shit and I better come pick it up before he sets fire to it. He's definitely not saying I'm Adele's mom.

"You couldn't tell the doctor fast enough that I was the nanny."

He grimaces. "I'm sorry. I wanted the doctor to know you aren't the biological mother in case she needed to know for blood tests or genetic reasons. I don't know. I was panicking."

"I was panicking, too. But I didn't accidentally call you an asshole."

"Swear jar," he mutters.

"This is a bar, not your house."

He growls. "Our home."

Oh, how I want his house to be my home. But he crapped all over that dream.

"Your house is not my home. You and I aren't together. And I quit my job as nanny."

"You are more than the nanny. I'm sorry I said you were. I don't react well when my baby girl is sick."

"I understand. I truly do." I get it. I was terrified for Adele, and she isn't mine to be terrified about. "But what happens the next time you panic? Adele is barely six months old. You have years of colds and cuts ahead. Not to mention all the trouble she'll get into once she's a teenager."

"My baby girl will never be in trouble."

"Did you forget she's a Raider? It's in her bones. She'll probably get detention in kindergarten for teaching the other children how to stage a protest."

He reaches for my hand but I retreat before he can touch me. He scowls. "This is why I need you. To help me raise her. To be her mommy."

"I can't do it, Zane. I'm not strong enough to handle you referring to me as the hired help the next time you panic."

I will not be my mom – accepting lousy seconds from a man. I deserve more.

"I will never refer to you as the hired help," he growls. "You're the woman I love. You're not some stranger I hired to watch my child."

I gasp. Zane loves me? Dare I hope he's being truthful? "Woman you love?"

"Yes, Sloane, you stubborn woman. I love you."

"But you never said."

"I tried to show you."

He did? "I didn't realize."

He smiles. "And I should have realized you didn't. I should have taken your past into consideration. It's not as if I'm not painfully aware of your past since your mother showed up twice."

I grimace. "Sorry."

"Don't you dare apologize for her. You have nothing to apologize for. You're amazing. Despite not having a dad or a mother worth the term, you're amazing." This time, when he reaches for me, I allow him to capture my hand. As we've established, I'm weak for this man.

"I love you, Sloane Wilder. Please put me out of my misery and say you'll come home."

"I don't know."

"It's fine. If you need time, I understand."

He does? He's not going to push me to accept what he wants? My desires be damned. "You do?"

"I love you. I plan to give you everything you ever need. Even if it's time when I'm impatient to have you back."

I give in. Let's face it. I was a goner the second he said he loves me. "Huh. I guess I'll come back since I love you and all."

His breath catches. "You love me?"

"Duh. Why do you think it hurt so bad when you called me the nanny?"

He draws me close. "I'll never call you the nanny again, sweetness. I love you."

He presses his lips against mine but Adele giggles and claps her hands before he can get to the good stuff. "Later," he promises against my lips.

"I'll hold you—"

"Get away from me, Miles Raider!" Hazel shouts.

I glance away from Zane to find Miles chasing after her.

Zane wraps an arm around my shoulders. "Let the show begin."

Happiness bursts from me. He apologized and admitted he was wrong. He didn't try to roll over my wishes and desires. He listened to me.

He's everything I've ever wanted and needed in a partner. I can't wait to start our lives together.

Chapter 37

Miles – a surfer who still hasn't figured out how to rectify the biggest mistake he made in his life

MILES

I glare at my phone when it rings. I contemplate ignoring it, but I'd only delay the inevitable. My brothers won't let me ignore them. They'll drag me by my ear if they have to. I'm not exaggerating. It wouldn't be the first time.

"Hey, Eli."

"Where are you?"

At home. Where I want to be.

When I don't answer, he sighs. "Shall I pick you up?"

"If I have to go, you do, too," Jaxon shouts.

Jaxon hates family occasions. He doesn't hate the Raider family. He just finds group outings stressful. He's a nerd who's proud to be an introvert. Being married to Blossom has made him more open to social occasions, but he's still an introvert.

Which means he's going to *Rumrunner* and there's no way I can bow out gracefully. I don't do anything gracefully, to be honest.

"Fine. Pick me up."

My house is in Smuggler's Rest. I can easily walk to *Rum-runner*. Hell, I can – and have – crawled there on occasion.

But I'm happy to hitch a ride since I don't want to go out tonight. Not when I know Hazel will be at the bar.

If you look up mistake in the dictionary, you'll find a picture of me. I messed up bad when I dumped Hazel back when I thought I was going to be a professional surfer and spend my life touring the world with my surfboard.

After I got injured in Hawaii, I slunk back to Smuggler's Hideaway with my tail between my legs. And – proving what a gigantic idiot I am – I didn't beg Hazel for forgiveness. Instead, I drowned myself in booze and women.

A car honks and I drag myself outside. Eli's SUV is already full but I squeeze between Blossom and Jaxon.

"Why can't you sit on the other side of me?" Jaxon asks.

"And miss you complaining?"

"I want to sit next to my wife."

"It's okay, nerd boy," Blossom says. "We'll get there faster if we don't have to all change seats."

Blossom isn't a nerd or an introvert the way Jaxon is, but she is obsessed with time management.

I throw my arm around her. "And this way, we get to become better acquainted."

Jaxon growls. "Keep your hands off my wife."

Blossom giggles. "He's just riling you up to get his mind off how Hazel will be at the bar."

I glare at her. "You're my least favorite sister-in-law."

"Technically, I'm your only sister-in-law since none of the other Raider brothers have gotten married yet. Engaged doesn't count."

I grunt. I don't understand how we got here. Every single one of my brothers is now paired off with a woman. Rhett, Eli, and Zane even have children.

A year ago, we were still those shit-stirring Raiders having fun, attending Mermaid karaoke, playing pranks on each other, and drinking way too much moonshine. I miss those days. It's no fun drinking by yourself, and the amount of pranks has slowed to a crawl.

We arrive at the bar and everyone piles out. Zane is standing at the alleyway waiting for us with his baby, Adele. Rhett and Dakota are standing next to him.

"Good," Zane says. "You're here." He makes his way toward the entrance of *Bootlegger.*

"I don't know why we're here," I whine.

Zane scowls at me. "I need your moral support."

"Whatever," I mutter and motion him forward.

We enter the bar. While Zane heads to the bartender to ask for Sloane, the rest of us shove tables together until there's enough room for all of the Raider family.

"I need a drink." I take everyone's orders before making my way to the bar.

On the way there, my gaze snags on red hair. Hazel must be a siren because my feet automatically change directions until I'm standing in front of her.

"What do you want?"

I blurt out the first thing I think of. "Can we talk?"

"Talk?" She snorts. "You don't want to talk. You never want to talk. You want to get into my pants and then forget all about it the next day."

"Not true." I can never forget about Hazel. I've spent the past weeks laying in bed imagining how it felt to have her in my arms again on New Year's Eve. How good she smelled. How crazy she goes for me when I kiss her lips.

My cock twitches. It remembers how it feels to be buried inside her.

"Not true? You're a liar. You're only interested in me when you're drunk. The rest of the time, you ignore me."

"I'm not drunk now."

She scans the room until her gaze falls on the Raider table, which is empty of drinks since I was supposed to order them.

"Fine." She crosses her arms over her chest and I can't avoid staring at her cleavage. It's magnificent. She's magnificent.

I reach for her and she scoots backwards. "I didn't give you permission to touch me."

I smirk. "You always do in the end."

Her green eyes flare with ire, and she shouts, "Get away from me, Miles Raider!"

She doesn't wait for me to move. She runs away. I give chase.

Chapter 38

"This is the chapter where forever begins."

A FEW WEEKS LATER

Zane

"Sloane," I groan as I climax.

I continue to glide in and out of her until my climax wanes. I pull out and she mewls. I feel the same way. Being buried inside of her is my favorite thing in the world. I'd stay there forever if I could.

I roll off of her and stroll to the bathroom. I get rid of the condom before returning to the bed. I slide in next to her and gather her in my arms.

"I'm sick of this shit."

She jerks in my hold. "I told you before. We can ditch the condoms."

I kiss her hair. "I'm not taking you bare until I've been tested."

Unfortunately, between Adele getting sick and being busy at work, I haven't had a chance to visit the doctor.

She glances up at me with trepidation in her dark brown eyes. I'm such an asshole. I put the trepidation there. I made her question my feelings for her. I planted doubt in her heart.

"Sweetness." I kiss her nose. "I promise I haven't been with anyone since you. Hell, I haven't been with anyone except you since Adele arrived."

"I know," she whispers.

"But…"

She frowns. "You haven't gotten tested. It's been weeks since you said I love you."

"When the hell have I had time?" I throw my arm out to indicate the loft she's still living in. "This is what I'm sick of. I'm sick of you sleeping here. I'm sick of dropping Adele at Mom's house so we can spend the night together."

"You can bring Adele here."

"Sweetness." I pinch her chin and force her to meet my gaze. "When you get off work at three in the morning and I finally have your attention for a few hours, I'm not distracting you with Adele."

Her nose wrinkles. "Distracting me?"

I grin. "You love Adele."

She rolls her eyes. "She's easy to love."

"And you miss her."

This is how I should have approached the issue – leaning on her love of Adele and her desire for a family is the way to Sloane's heart.

She sighs. "I do."

Instead of Sloane caring for Adele each day while I work, I now bring my baby girl to daycare. When I get off work, I spend the evening with my daughter. Then, I sleep for a few hours before dragging my ass out of bed to spend time with Sloane.

"If you were living with me, you could spend every morning with her."

"Zane," she growls.

"Don't you dare tell me it's too early to live together. I love you. I want you in my bed every night. I'm fucking done with not waking up with you in my arms each morning."

She melts in my arms. "I enjoy waking up in your arms, too."

"Good. Let's stop this two houses shit, and you move back in with me. Back home where you belong."

"I'm…" She trails off and nibbles her lip.

I remove her lip from her teeth. "You're what?" When she hesitates, I push. "Come on, sweetness. Tell me why you're hesitating to take what you want."

"How do you know what I want is to live with you?"

"Sweetness."

"Fine. It is. But you don't have to be smug about it."

"How can I not be smug? I managed to get the woman I love to love me, despite my past, despite what an idiot I was. I'm the shit."

She slaps my shoulder. "You're too humble for your own good."

I snatch her hand and place it against my heart. Her eyes widen when she feels how fast my heart is beating.

"Are you… nervous?"

"Hell, yeah, I am. I fucked up with you. I should have handled you with the utmost care. I should have made sure you never doubted my love for you. I didn't. And now I'm worried I can't repair what I broke."

"I'll move in."

I blink. "What?"

"Zane." She places her palm on my cheek. "You admitted to your mistakes. Mom…" She blows out a breath. "She never thinks anything is her fault. If she has to blame anyone, she blames me. I want a partner who will own up to his faults and work on fixing things. That's you."

Relief courses through me. Sloane forgives me. She said she did weeks ago but she's been cautious.

"No more caution? No more hesitation?"

Her smile stretches from ear to ear. It's a beautiful smile. She's beautiful. She's fucking perfect.

"No more caution. Although." She narrows her eyes at me. "I expect you to make time for a doctor's appointment pronto."

"I'll go this morning. After we move your shit back into our home."

I press my lips to hers, but when she reaches for me, I slip out of her hold. "No time for that. We're packing you up now."

She giggles. "Zane, it's four in the morning."

"Don't care."

"I love you. You're crazy, but I love you."

"I love you, too, sweetness." I smack her ass. "Now, get moving."

"I'm not moving in the middle of the night. Can you imagine what the gossipers will say?" She shivers and I give in. The town will gossip no matter what we do, but I don't want her to feel embarrassed in any way.

"What are we going to do in the meantime?"

She feigns a yawn. "I'm tired."

"You're not tired."

She bats her eyelashes at me. "I worked a ten-hour shift. My feet hurt, and my back is aching."

"Roll over," I order.

"Why?"

"Roll over and I'll show you why."

"Why, Zane Raider, are you going to seduce me?"

My cock hardens and lengthens at her husky voice. I growl as I crawl on top of her. "As often as you'll let me."

"This idea sounds interesting. Let's explore this more."

She wraps her legs around me. I can feel her hard nipples press against my chest and her warm heat against my cock. I'm done talking. It's time for action.

"Talking is done. Time to show you how much I love you."

"Yes, please."

I meld my lips to hers before I proceed to show her how much I love her. I'll show her I love her every day for the rest of my life. Until the last breath leaves my body. She's mine. I'm hers. Together, we're going to grow our small family into the loud, rambunctious family she's always dreamed of. Whatever she wants, she's getting.

Starting with an orgasm.

About the author

D.E. Haggerty is an American who has spent the majority of her adult life abroad. She has lived in Istanbul, various places throughout Germany, and currently finds herself in The Hague. She has been a military policewoman, a lawyer, a B&B owner/operator and now a writer.

Printed in Dunstable, United Kingdom

78312681R00170